you are my best friend, you are my world
you don't understand, you know i love you,
you never listen, you want, it's always you

whanau

you only ever yell at me, you never listen,

Whanau

stories of family, friends, fears and faith

Published by Hallard Press
Papakura
Aotearoa/New Zealand
2013

ISBN 978-0-9876529-7-3

Whanau means family in Maori, the indigenous language of Aotearoa. Whanau is one of a series of collected short stories. Some of the stories within this series have appeared in other collections or publications. Others are published for the first time. This is the first time all have been brought together in one collection.
Whanau is also available as a Kindle ebook.

Cover and inside design Hallard Press.
Covers and inside photography - Stock footage provided by elvinstar / Pond5.com
The persons depicted are models and their likeness is being used for illustrative purposes only.

CONTENTS

there'll be a time
when my grief
will loose words
like armed men
on those I love

RIWAI

"Then I got it all worked out," said old aunty Heeni. "That old kuia musta been collecting up bits of my hairs and finger nails and all that so she could makutu me, and then I have to go with - you know - that nephew of hers. I was scared! I run out of that tent fast, not getting my gears or nothing. I get on the bus. And back home! And do you know what I heard ... "

I got up and walked out and left them all listening to her. I just couldn't take any more of that. I hoped she'd think I was going for a mimi. But I caught the look she threw me as I went out the door. She knew.

She calls me her riwai - her potato. You get the idea? Brown on the outside, white and hard and cold on the inside. That really hurts, more than any names you could call me. When she's in a good mood she sometimes might call me "bread" - same idea, you know? Then she'd say, "But might be in time we can fry her or toast her all to brown, eh?"

But I just do not want to know any of that stuff she was in there telling them. All this about ghosts and spirits and makutu and the old ones of the dead looking over your shoulder all the time. And tapu. God, I remember when she told me about some distant cousin of hers who'd wandered - when she was still a kid, mind you - onto some place she'd been told to keep off because it was an old burial ground. And the kid had fallen down a sand bank and wound up lying on top of a bone that had been exposed in the fall. And she'd suddenly known for certain that her own bones had come from that bone and she was breaking terribly a tapu. And her hand had sort of frozen to the bone like she had an electric shock for a long time. Then she'd run home bawling and shivering. Her blood had seemed to turn to wax in her veins and her lungs to paper. She'd died in a few weeks mumbling with madness.

I just can't stand that kind of thing. I had nightmares for days after hearing that one. I get a cold shiver right down inside my backbone if ever I let my mind turn to those things. Old Heeni believes it all. To her it's the heart of being a Maori. Not me, though. That's not my line. I'm not that sort of Maori.

I wanted now to get my head clear of what I'd had to hear that day from her. But, too, I wanted to think about what uncle Pita had said. No, not *her* husband, not Heeni's - he's a bit too young for that. No, my father's uncle Pita. That's why Heeni was here. Pita had wanted to see us. No, I've got to be honest - to see me. And that's what I had to think about. It was really important.

"You," uncle Pita had said to me just that morning, "you have the best education of us all, of all this whole family."

I guessed he didn't mean only us sitting there. "Oh come on," I said, "I'm going for my Year 13 NCEA, that's all. What about Rita?"

"Rita is too far away. And anyway, she's no good with a twin baby on each side of her for what we want. No, you are the one. Here is the time now to put your education to use for us, your family. Now is the time for your Maori heart to show itself."

Me the best educated one in the family? Even Rita just had her NCEA. Well, yes, I suppose. You see, we're a poor lot - in money, I mean. Our land, our family land, is way back in the sticks so far you'd never believe it. And what a mix-up of a history. First it got confiscated - you know, the Maori wars. Then when the government found out where it was and someone took a look they gave it back. But no one would ever lend any money for a long time to help turn it into half-way decent farms. Even now it's a hard case lot of land. Most Pakeha farmers'd chuck it in the sea and go off somewhere else. Uncle Pita's son, he's the only one farming it now. He pays all the rest of us some bit of rent for the use of the land as a sheep run. But even he can't break in all those gullies and hills and so.

But - now here's the thing - when he was starting out he managed to get a loan to develop the place. And now they wanted the loan repaid - only he hasn't got the money. And we, our family, stand to lose our only bit of land.

And now all this was on my plate. I got the cold sweats to think of it. This was just too much. But uncle Pita wouldn't let me wriggle out of it. "I'm too young," I said, "to solve this problem."

"Maybe," he said, his eyes staring straight into mine.

"But if you aren't used to talking to these Pakehas by now, who is? You got the words and the jaw to talk back to them, you know what they mean. If I take my boys in there with me or your father, they'll just let those fullas in the insurance walk all over them with rugby boots. It's your job, Ani, and you'll go with me."

And so there was me with old uncle Pita in the office in the insurance company, with all its modern plastic furniture and window drapes and a carpet (so thick!), and a man sitting there with a face that looked like it wouldn't know what sun was. And little gold wire glasses that caught the light so you couldn't see his eyes. And so calm and polite. While I could feel right beside me uncle Pita getting hotter and hotter and hating his guts. And me, I was sweating too, you bet.

"I'm sorry," said the man, "but these are bad times for us all."

Oh yeah!

"We simply cannot afford you another extension. Look again at the figures," and he shoved the print-out at me for the umpteenth time. "The current rate of repayment is simply not reducing the initial capital advance fast enough. You know that your family was really on very advantageous terms originally. And you have enjoyed several extensions to date."

This was really getting above my head. But I had to make an effort for the family's sake. I hung on to all I'd learned about accountancy and economics and such.

"How about if the rate of repaying the loan was increased?" I said. "Would that mean you could let the loan stay for a while longer? Maybe the farm could afford a few more dollars a week repayment."

"Yes, yes," uncle Pita nodded proudly, "that is a sound idea my niece has. We pay you more and you leave us a bit longer to repay your loan."

But the guy was shaking his head. "I'm sorry, Mr Manihera," he said, "but that is out of the question. Not only is it our firm policy to recall these very long-term loans and bring all loans into line with the requirements of the current economic situation. But the balance sheet of your property simply will not allow for any such increase in outgoing payments."

"So when do you want the loan paid back by?" I asked.

I was giving up.

"They want the Maoris' land," my uncle hissed to me. "All the rest is lies. They have found a use for the land, you'll see. They'll take the land if we cannot pay back their loan on time."

"We can give you six months until final settlement," said the fulla.

"And you can't give us another loan to use to pay this one?" I asked again.

"I regret that as I said your family's economic circumstances would not permit the raising of a fresh loan at current rates."

"What will you do with the land if we have to give it up?" I said. Nothing to lose by trying to find out why they were trying to ease us off the land.
"That is not my department," said the man smooth as you like.
"Well, I'll get back to you. See what we can do," I told him, just to give him the idea we weren't beat yet.
"Oh yes, it would be such a pity to lose that property after it has been so long in your family," said the guy.
"Six hundred years we have held it," said uncle Pita.
"So long as that, fancy that now," said the 'keha without batting an eyelid.
"Well, my accountancy didn't work," I remarked to uncle Pita as we went down about a thousand floors in the lift.
"Try now your history," he said. And wouldn't explain.

Now I'm sitting here, my head pounding I've thought and worried so long. Trouble is, I know exactly what to do. Sure, it's all in the history books, it's been done before. The family think the land is useless - it doesn't grow a subsistence amount of crops. That's why they just run sheep over it and no one hardly lives there. But a teacher's told me - and showed me maps to prove it - that the soil's no different from places further down the coast where they do market gardening. All you need is to add the special trace elements to the soil and get a truck to cart the produce. Cropping the place - potatoes maybe - could bump the profits way up. And get a loan somewhere else - these teachers here, they've told me where to try. Payoff that smoothie shark at the insurance firm. But it'd be hard slog. No rest. As many of us as possible on the land there the next year or two. Seven days a week, I guess.
And who'd be the work gang boss? You've got it. Old soft hands, me. So that's my choice: stay at school, maybe get my exams, get me a good job. Or chuck school and save our papakainga (sure, they say there was a marae there once), our turangawaewae back up country just about as far as you can get from this city, with the old peeling house and outdoor loo and a dirt road and a TV that makes the programmes look like old Heeni's ghost stories.
Okay, you tell me what to do.
Yeah, and whatever I do, I'm still going to be aunty Heeni's riwai, you can bet on it!

FAMILY

I finished the comic and chucked it back to Joyce. The teacher now had her back to us and was writing some stuff on the blackboard. I stood up and had a look out the window. It was a really sunny day out there. My stomach rumbled. Boy, I was starved. So I got up and walked out the door. I think I heard the teacher calling out as I went round the corner of the building, but I didn't look back to find out. It was warm outside, but I didn't take my leather jacket off.

I had no money again. Not to worry. I went across the playing field at the back of the school, over the fence, and down to the shops. In the supermarket I helped myself to some packets of chips, some cakes, a coke and some other stuff and put them all in a big paper bag. I waited till the checkouts were busy, then I walked out where you come into the shop. Five finger free, eh. Easy.

I decided to go round to Kimi's place. I'd heard they had a new big flash TV. I found George there too, the both of them sitting back watching the telly - yeah it was a big mother flatscreen job - drinking a beer each. But it was only some dopey show with talking heads. So Kimi turned it off. 'You off school again today?' said George. I didn't answer him. He and Kimi were both unemployed - so they could talk. We were talking away when Kimi shot up out of his chair. 'Oh hell,' he said, staring out the window. I turned around. There was a cop car pulled up outside. 'They're coming here,' said Kimi and threw a glance at the TV. Oh no! George was on his feet, too, spilling beer down his jeans. 'We got to get out of here,' he was saying. Boy, they were in a state. He started to make for the back door. I could just picture it: a cop was bound to be out back in a moment in time to spot him and give chase. 'Oh come on,' I said. I knew Kimi's house well - it was like ours. I led them at a run out the back door and right into the back door of the unit that was bang up against theirs. 'Hi, Mrs,' I told the surprised lady as we rushed past her and into a bedroom and out the open window, and over the fence into the next section. I strolled down the fence and looked back to Kimi's. A cop was just going into the house. No one else was around. 'Come on,' I called to them, and we shot over the back fence and around the next block of flats and down the grass behind the whole line of them until we got to a street.

'We did that good,' said George, laughing and trying to slap both our shoulders with only one hand. The idiot was still clutching his empty can in his other hand.
'OK, OK,' said Kimi. He was looking mean. I think he got a bit of a shrink that we'd cut out and run like that. But we all kept on walking, putting a real tangle of streets between us and his place.
'Well, you can't go back there a while, man,' said George. 'Where you going to lay low?'
I could almost see Kimi going down the list of places. 'I dunno,' he said at last. 'They know all my places by now.'
'Well, you can't come to my place. My old man doesn't even want me around there anymore, he reckons,' said George. He chucked the empty can into the gutter. And just as if the clatter had sprung a trigger, an idea hit me. 'I've got it,' I said. 'Come on,' and led them along at a fair clip. We had a fair way to go.
This state house had been empty a long time. The grass was about half a metre high, and rags of dirty curtains hung in the windows. I shoved hard at the door. Hey, it was still unlocked. Inside was a funny smell and it was real stuffy. And there were some cupboards off their hinges and a door propped up against the wall, and the wallpapers were hanging down in strips. But it wasn't too bad. There was a light bulb in one of the rooms - and, yes, the power was on. Even Kimi was grinning. 'Eh, this'll do, Pita boy.'
'Tonight,' I told them, 'each of us get some stuff from home or somewhere so we can set this place up. You know, mattresses, cushions, something to eat off, some food and such.' Because I had suddenly decided to move in there too. I was betting to myself that the house had been overlooked in some office, it had been left alone such a long time.
When I told Mum I was moving in for a while with the others, she just said, 'So long as you know what you're doing. Don't get into any trouble with those mates of yours.' But the old lady was really too busy to pay me much mind. Dad was on the booze again - she'd have her hands full when he got home. But the other older kids could help her with him this time if he got punchy. The little'uns were a bit hacked off that I wouldn't give them any of the shrapnel like I usually did when I had money in my hand. But I reckoned we'd need all the cash we could lay our hands on to keep us fed. Because all sorts of ideas were running

through my head about what we could do with this house we'd taken over.

When I got back to the house and dumped all the stuff I'd got out of the shopping trolley I'd found down our street, I noticed a little kid playing. She was about five or six, I'd say. 'Hullo,' she said, 'this is my new house. Are you visiting us?'

'Eh?'

Kimi spoke up. 'I brought her along. My cousin's supposed to look after her while her mother's away, but she and her husband've gone off too.'

'Look, we can't really look after her, can we?' Kimi just shrugged. The little girl was looking at me anxiously. Boy! 'Oh all right,' I said.

'Come here,' I said to her, 'this'll be your room.' And showed her the smallest bedroom at the back of the house.

Just then in walked George. He had his girl with him. 'Listen,' he said, 'Jeanette's moving in here too.'

Kimi got off the floor and grinned at her. I'll admit I gave her a looking over too. But she was more interested in talking to the little kid.

'We'll have this room here,' said George, and started to tell her to cart their gear into the front bedroom.

'Hold it,' I said. I was thinking like fury. This was a whole new ball game. George stopped dead and frowned at me. 'Huh?'

'We're not having a honeymoon hotel here,' I told him.

Kimi grinned and his eyes slid round to Jeanette again. 'Let's lay it on the line,' I told them, 'we got to play it cool. No pairing off like that. Not yet anyway. We've got to establish ourselves, we're not going to risk any trouble among ourselves. And we've got to show the neighbours we're OK. They've got to think we're here by rights, eh. You understand? In a way, though, it's good Jeanette's here. Makes it look more like a normal household. OK, OK. And someone's got to look after that kid while she's here, and Jeanette can do that. Right? Jeanette and the kid in the back room. Two of us in the front and one in the other bedroom. '

'Not worth,' said George, a real sulk on his face, because he could see Kimi agreed with me.

'Oh yes it is.' We all looked in surprise at how firmly Jeanette spoke up. 'Pita's got it right. I need somewhere to go and I'm staying here even if you're not,' she told George. Kimi was going to snigger but I glared him to silence. George glowered for a minute. Then he said, 'That's

how you want it. Just for now, mind you.' And carted stuff out and we could hear his boots walking into the bedroom at the back.
'And you lay off her too,' I said to Kimi when Jeanette and the kid went off to set up their room.
'Oh yeah?' he said, getting heavy. I went right up to him. 'Yeah,' I said. Kimi could see what I wanted to remind him of - how even though he was a year or two older than me my shoulders stuck out on either side of his and how he had to look up a little to meet my eye. He decided to make a joke. 'Sure father,' he said, 'it's just us monks and nuns here.'
That day was pretty busy. I trotted in next door to make friendly with the lady of that house, taking Jeanette and the kid with me. I spun the lady a story about how we were all brothers and sisters and relatives and how our parents were moving in just as soon as my father had finished his job. I don't know how much the lady believed, but she was friendly and she didn't ask too many questions.
'You got a fast imagination,' Jeanette told me on our way back. 'You could write stories!'
'Teachers always say my stories are junk,' I told her.
'What do they know?' she said.
Then I took Kimi down with me and blew all our cash on supplies. And by the time we returned we found the family had got another member. It was Sam, sort of cousin of mine on the Pakeha side, and like me still going to high school. A pretty useless kid, all he could think of was discos. Lazy sod, too. But how could I turn my cousin out when I knew he'd got so much hassle at home?
Then I got us organised. I called a meeting and allocated jobs. (Funny that, come to think of it, no one else wanted to take over the job of acting as boss.) 'We've each got to have our jobs, otherwise the place'll fall apart. OK? First, me and Sam. Our big job is to go to school.'
'Doubt it!' Sam was shocked.
'We have to. We don't want the school or the truant people round here, do we? You just make sure you're there every day, boy.
'You're worse than me old man,' Sam sulked.
'Your choice if you stay,' I said, but I knew he would. 'But, listen,' I told him, 'I'll go round to your home and say you're staying with us and getting to school.'
Sam looked more hopeful at that. 'OK,' he agreed. 'Sam and me,' I went on, 'we're the general dog's bodies, to help where we're needed. Now, you two fullas, you on the unemployment? '

Neither answered.

'Well?'

'Ah - we haven't got round to it yet,' said George.

'You can get it?' I asked.

'Suppose,' said Kimi.

'Well then, you just get round there today and fill in those forms. We've got to have money coming in.'

'Yeah, but what if they offer us some crummy job?' said George.

'You take it,' I said. I must've looked fed up because no one said anything to that. Those two just scowled. 'Jeanette, you'll look after the cooking, housekeeping, mind this kid. Right?'

'OK,' she said. 'I've also got a part-time job - three days a week ten o'clock to four.'

'Good girl,' I told her.

'But she was going to throw it in,' protested George. 'It's a boring job. And we-'

I glared at him. 'I'll keep it on,' said Jeanette. I really liked that girl. She was worth all those other three fullas together. 'Now, Kimi, your job is to go down to the workers' co-op down the road each time they go into the city markets and you can go help them and get us some foods and so.'

'What?' He was puzzled.

'You know, they bid for the stuff - call out the prices they'll pay.'

'I got it, right,' he said, 'I'm in business, hey how do you fullas like that?'

'George, your job is to get the grass down and get the place looking like it's lived in.'

'Not me!'

'Just you,' I said. 'Otherwise we'll have the people around to fix the place - and that'll fix us. We've got to fool them that the place is lived in and that everything's OK. You got it?'

'Come on, George,' said Jeanette pressing up to him.

'Just for a while then,' he said.

There was silence. Everyone looked glum. 'Bloody hard work this'll be,' said Kimi at last. 'How did we get into all this?'

'You knocked off a TV,' said George.

The little kid was sitting on the floor right by me staring up at me. I'd forgotten all about her. 'And you, Melanie, you'll help with the dishes and the housework - and you'll be the chief shopper. Can you do all that?'

She smiled at me. 'I can do those things just easy,' she said.

Good kid that one.

George spoke up. 'If we get caught short of money we can lift stuff, eh.'

'Yeah, and if you get nicked you'll do for us all,' said Sam.

A couple of days later, our first Friday in the place, came the event I'd been half expecting. The gang Kimi belonged to came to call. The Urban Guerillas they called themselves. Real smart heads. There was a racket outside about nine or ten o'clock at night, and Kimi marched in.

'Me mates have come for a piss up,' he said.

'Not here, they won't,' I said.

'That's what they're going to do, a house warming, eh,' said Kimi and started to swagger out the house. I slammed the door in front of him. 'There's going to be no house breaking here,' I told him, 'because that's about all the gorillas' ideas'd be.' There was a tremendous kicking on the door. I flung it open, weighed up the guy who was doing it in my mind, and suddenly straight armed him. He hit hard on the concrete path. Jeanette was right behind me looking scared. 'Get into your room and shut the door,' I told her. I went out to where the leader was lounging on the gatepost. The members crowded me in. 'Look, Aka,' I told him, 'we just can't have yous fullas here.' And I explained to him how if anyone rang for the police around here we'd all of us be for it, and especially Kimi. I watched him carefully. I was ready to take him on, even though I knew he'd drop me. He thought for a while. 'You got a point,' he said. 'See ya. Come on yous guys.' He nodded to someone, then turned round and walked off. There was a bit of bad-tempered kicking at the door and pounding on the windows, and then they straggled off after him. Kimi, surly faced, went after them. 'What cha do that for? I've had a guts full of you, fella,' he hissed as he went past me. Suddenly something slammed into my ear and I staggered. It was the guy I'd knocked down, and on each side of me was a gorilla making sure I gave no trouble. He gave me another swipe at the face, and drew blood. Then they went. It was a small price to pay. I found George and Sam and Jeanette on the step. 'Just, you know, in case,' mumbled George as we went in.

We'd got rid of the gang, but other people kept on drifting in and out, and bringing their grog and so. When I got up on Monday morning I found a couple of extras who'd apparently moved in with us. But they were just too lazy to get home, so I heaved them out into the street.

It was a tough week. We had two members of the family in the sulks. Kimi because he considered I'd shamed him in front of the gang. And Sam because I wouldn't fork out money for the disco. I told him we had to eat before he danced. With Jeanette home in the mornings, George didn't do much garden work by the look of the place till I told him to cut out the funny stuff and get busy. But the kid's mother finally arrived to take her home, so that was one less problem. We were short of money till I told Kimi and George to ask for the emergency money you can get if you're broke. You had to tell those two every damned thing. I was so tired a couple of times I dropped off to sleep in class. But by the end of the week things were going fairly smoothly. Kimi started to bring his girl round, but she didn't want to move in. Good thing too, I was finding just us quite enough. By the weekend the grass was more or less cut with the neighbour's mower, the house was quite clean and comfortable, we'd got enough food laid in, and we even had some cash in hand. And then Kimi arrived with a TV. 'Relax,' he said, 'I've borrowed it off a friend. Mind you, I didn't ask how come they'd got two.' We were in clover.

I was pretty proud of us. We were becoming a real family, this girl, two high school kids and two unemployed and - on and off - the little kid who kept turning back up when her useless mum was on the booze. Every few days someone else would stop over for the night. But I was determined no one was going to move in permanently unless they had a good need, and unless they could fit in with us.

I came home from school one afternoon to find Sam had a little man who looked like a salesman waiting for me in the house. 'He's got a job for me,' Sam said. The fulla looked surprised to see me, he was probably expecting to deal with a father or someone like that. I didn't trust him as soon as I saw him.

'You boys make your own decisions, eh?' he asked. I nodded. 'Well then,' he was very businesslike all of a sudden. 'Sam will do a few simple jobs for me a few nights every month. Good pay. Sorry I can't offer you a job, too, Pete.'

'Pita. What job will he do?'

The guy explained vaguely. Suddenly I saw daylight. 'You mean he helps break in schools and places and nicks stuff for you? Not on your life.'

The guy turned nasty. 'Reckon you're not in any position to stop it,' he said. He glanced round the place. 'Interesting set up here,' he said, hint, hint.
I thought I saw how to handle this. I yelled for Kimi to come in. The guy's face went a paler shade when he made out the Guerillas' sign.
When Kimi heard the man's plans he simply cocked his thumb at the door. 'Out,' he said.
'Now you just look here-'
'Forget us and him,' Kimi nodded at Sam. The guy hustled out of the house.
'Nice one,' I told Kimi.
Sam was yelling with fury. 'You've loused up my chance to grab the money.'
Kimi yanked Sam's shirt. 'Don't,' I said.
'You want me to get bloody bored to death?' shouted Sam.
'Good job too,' said Kimi and went out. And there was no more trouble with Sam on that one.
An afternoon or two later I was stretched out on my mattress looking over some comics. (I'd sneaked home from school - it was only a sportsday or some such.) Jeanette came in and sat down right by me. She was looking good. There was something different about her. 'New blouse,' she said.
'Ahuh,' I said.
'I've been round home,' she said. 'Things seem not too bad now. But I'm going to stay on. I like it here.'
I felt relieved. It'd be tough without her. 'That's good,' I responded.
'There's a good feeling here now,' she went on.
She was looking at me really hard. Her eyes' pupils were so dark you could hardly see the little black spot in the centre. I was getting uncomfortable because I felt warmly towards her myself. It wasn't just that she was fairly pretty, it was also that I liked her. But, hell, I wouldn't risk starting trouble in the family even over her.
'George'll be glad you're staying,' I said. (Even though I still hadn't let him move in with her. After all, that was the room we put any girls who wanted to stay over, or the little kid whenever she drifted back.)
'Maybe,' she said. 'But I reckon him and me are about through, eh.'
I said nothing.
'It's not him I'm staying for,' she said.
I said nothing, but glanced down at a comic.

'Can't you see what I'm saying?' She sounded really wild.
I sighed. 'I'm not that dumb,' I said, 'and I like you too.'
She smiled. And came up closer. I shoved her back. 'But you've got to sort this out with George. I'm not looking for trouble like that in this place. You understand?'
Well, she decided to sort it out that same evening. George came home a bit liquored up from going to the pub with some mates. They shut themselves in her room, but they needn't have bothered. Everyone down the road could hear. I went out and left them to it. Couldn't think what else to do. I wondered if this was the biggest test of our family yet. That night I came back late and next day I made sure I kept well away from Jeanette. But George was looking only a little surly. Maybe she'd had the sense not to bring my name into it. But all that day I felt like I was walking on hot hangi stones. By the end of that evening I breathed easier - maybe we'd passed through that test. I allowed myself a smile - maybe at last, life was going to be sweet. And I found I couldn't wait for tomorrow when me and Jeanette, perhaps, could start to get together. Need to stay cool, not rush, not unsettle George. But yeah, maybe.
Next morning we were just having something for breakfast when a guy appeared right in the kitchen. 'What's all this?' he demanded. We had the little kid with us again, and she backed up tight against the wall.
'What's this with you in our house?' I said, getting up.
A second guy appeared. You could see straight away this one was from the welfare. You can tell their sort a mile off, eh. I looked out the window, but I couldn't see any police with them. The first guy's eyes were skittering around like flies, looking really suspicious and mean.
'What are you all doing here?' said the welfare fulla.
'You're squatters on government property,' put in the other man.
'You've no right to be here.'
I could see Kimi opening his mouth so I broke in quickly.
'Who has the right to be here then?' I asked.
'No one,' said the guy, 'absolutely no one.'
'We aren't doing any harm,' said Jeanette.
'Oh really?' he said, moving his head around to look at the smashed cupboards and the wallpaper.
'Hey, that's not us,' said George.
'That's not the point,' said the welfare man.

'Now you,' pointing to Sam, 'what are you doing here? Why aren't you at home?'
'This is my home,' replied Sam.
The guy made a noise in his nose.
'This is our family,' I said. 'We are looking after ourselves, our families know we're here-'
'We got a regular income coming in,' said George proudly. They looked suspicious at that.
'You've got to get out of here,' the first guy said impatiently. 'You could be in serious trouble just moving in like this.'
'Are you wanting a rent from us?' I asked him.
'Don't you get cheeky, young lad,' he said. 'I'm just wanting all of you out off these premises here and now.'
'And I want to know exactly what's been going on here,' said the welfairy, eyeing Jeanette and the kid. 'What's she doing here?' he said looking at Melanie. 'And how old are you?' he said to me, 'And what are you doing here?' he said to Kimi.
'Living,' said Kimi.
'And I'll get the police in if I have to,' the first guy was carrying on. He'd read the gang emblem on Kimi's jacket.
'You're going to break our family up?' I asked the welfare guy. I still couldn't quite believe what was going on.
'You're a fool if you do, this is the only place any of us have ever been safe, ever done some decent work,' said Jeanette, cuddling the kid. And I looked across at her standing there, with the kid, and I felt this surge inside, proud of her, but also, I could all of a sudden see this future for me, not like anything I had imagined before - me, her, a kid, a house, a family. And it was all now maybe not going to happen.
The welfare guy's eyes looked over us all. He gathered up the other fulla, who was still muttering at us, and they went back outside, stood next to their car and had a consult together. And here we are. Our family, looking at each other, maybe for the last time - waiting for the authorities to decide if we get to keep living together in, like Jeanette said, the only place we've ever felt right, the place we made ourselves, or get thrown back into the world, their world, the world of shit and blame and wrong.
And I realised that all their eyes were suddenly on me. Looking at me. Expecting me to come up with the thing that would save us all. And what could I do?

A CALL TO MY DAUGHTER

The phone rings. "Hullo," the voice of my daughter says to me. I'm at once afraid. "Has anything happened?" I ask. "Why are you phoning? Is it about my grandson?"
"Just ringing," she says, "to say I've shifted."
"Shifted?" I'm not sure what she is trying to tell me.
"Yes. Out of the flat. I've left that man, and for good this time."
I don't reveal to her how greatly she has shaken my feelings. All I can says is, "That makes me sad, Ima."
"I had to do it," she says, "you know how he beat me."
I reminded her gently, "It wasn't so bad."
She is silent, she won't speak to me. But I think it's more important now that she listens. I ask, "Was what you suffered so different from what so many of us women put up with? Go back, and –"
"No! I can't," she cuts into my words. "Please, Mum, don't tell him where I am."
"You haven't told your own mother where it is you've shifted to."
She pauses. And I know that there's something she hesitates to tell me.
"Ima?"
"Mum, I've moved to Dunedin."
I'm so amazed, I'm so confused, I put down the phone. I've heard of that city in the South Island where hardly any Samoans live.
I've heard there are only men who have to be apprentices down there, so far away, so close to the South Pole it makes me shiver to think about it.
And I'm cold, cold with sorrow for my daughter. What I've most dreaded since we came to this country at last is happening. I can't hold my tears. Ima, Ima, I look at you and see my sister. You are beautiful, clever. But you'd rather have penguins for your family than your own a'iga?

I ring her up. I find out from the phone book how to do it. It takes a long time for them to find her telephone number. "Ima, you can't do this."
"Mum, please don't feel that way. I just have to be away from my husband."

"I'm thinking of my grandson also," I tell her sharply. "Vai needs a family, he needs all of us. He needs a man."
"I don't want him to grow up seeing his mother beaten, learning to put his temper into his fists – "
"That's our way." I speak loudly to make her hear. "Vai has to learn to look after himself. We've accepted what sometimes happens to us because of that, us women, for a very long time."
"No, mum – "
"You're like a little girl, Ima, about this."
"I won't accept it," she says. "Nor will my son."
I speak slowly and clearly into the blind white face of this telephone. "Listen to me. You'll turn your back on the good things, too, of our people's life, it's all connected together. Who can choose just this or that? Haven't you ever understood, Ima?"

As I work in my house I try to think how I can help my daughter and my grandson. All I can think of is my fear for them. She is removing herself, she seems determined to remove herself from her family. I ask and ask myself, Why does she want to keep her child from us? Doesn't she understand that distance finally becomes distance in the spirit?
I phone her. "How is Vai?"
"He's recovering," she says
The phone seems to leap against my clasp "Something has happened to my grandson?"
"It's his arm," she says. "An accident. A car bumped into him."
"A car? How could you let a car run over him?"
"Mum, please be calm. He's all right. It's only a fracture."
"Which hospital is he in?" I ask.
"He's home now. He has plaster on it and he's healing. But it will take a while. It's just that the doctor thinks it might be a bit shorter than the other arms because of the type of fracture."
I cannot speak for a moment. Then I have to explain it to her, she can see nothing for herself. "It's God's will."
"No, no," she says. She is crying now. Her heart is softening?
"It's your punishment for treating your promises to God in your marriage like a thing that you buy in a shop and throw it away."
"Please, mum, don't say that," she says, "how can you say that?"
"Speak Samoan," I tell her, "speak our language to me. This is our family we're talking about."

"How can you say these things?" She is taking no notice of me. "What has Vai done to be punished? He's a little child."
"Yes," I want to make the matter clear to her. "Yet – "
"What have I done to cause Vai to have his arm broken?"
My cold sorrow at her hardness grows. But I say nothing. Oh Vai, my grandson, deformed because your mother ran from us and from your father. I am wounded in the heart.

"Is Vai well?" I enquire when I phone her next.
"I told you," she says, "the doctor says it will be a month before he's completely recuperated, before he can use his arm properly."
"Come back here," I plead, "come to us, let us look after him."
"That man would find me again," she says, she is obsessed. "He'd use Vai to force me to live with him. I can't go through that again."
I think of what my little Vai is going through.

When I ring her again my husband speaks to her. "Your mother and I will come down to Dunedin and see you both."
"That makes me happy," she tells him. "Can you stay with cousin Pat's friend?"
"Pat's friend? Why should we stay with a stranger?" asks my husband. "We'll stay with you. It's you we're coming to see, not them.
"I'm living in a little flat," she answers him. "I've only this one room and this one bed Vai and I have to share."
My husband is angry. "Let her freeze!" he says to me. "She will have nothing to do with us." He doesn't mean it. He loves her so much that he becomes angry with her.

I ring her. "Your father's eldest brother, our matai, doesn't want to see you when he comes to New Zealand next month. You have shamed the a'iga. They've heard even in Samoa of the girl who's left her husband, who lives on her own in a different city, who won't have anything to do with her family."
She grunts. That's what it sounds like. She grunts over the phone to her mother, like a pig's this noise of hers. She is like the papalagi say it, Pig head. "Don't use that pig head voice to me," I tell her.

"Oh mum, please don't growl at me all the time." She sounds like a little girl again. "My life's been a hell," she says. "I've been crazy with worry as it is."

I am so shocked that I have to tell her, "Don't speak that way."

But she's not hearing me, she's going on, "I've had enough troubles to cope with, with Vai being hurt, and with trying to make ends meet."

"Come –"

She continues, "I've only lately stopped limping from what he did to me."

"Come home to us!"

"No, mum. I'm beginning to make a life here."

My heart is in pain. I will pray to God to bring back my daughter to us, to move her soul to recognise what is right. "Oh my daughter, when can we be one in heart again?" But I've already put down the phone.

She needs help. Even her angry words cry out to me that she needs all of us, that she knows she is part of the family whatever happens. Yet some evil fights in her against what she's been taught. My torn daughter.

I will not have my grandson Vai brought up to be a foreigner to me, and to the ways of his ancestors.

Would he go, that husband of hers, would he go and try it again with her – if he found out her hiding place? I think so. Ima, you mother's love hears your agony, will help. Soon, soon, you'll find out how.

TRUST

I'm always telling her I love her, but I'm too crazy for her. All our people are crazy, our terrible lives have made us that way, we're not safe for people like her. It's so hard for us to hold thoughts together.

She wants to know about my life, why I am here. I can't tell her, I won't go through it all again even for her, the life we had, the government hunting us, sending tanks rolling over villages and towns, and other people fighting us because of religion and ideas, Christians Muslims Socialists who cares what they call themselves, all of them butchers, assassins, liars, puffed up Alexanders.

I find one tiny small story to share with her, perhaps she'll understand something from it.

My family are at a meal one day and we hear neighbours yelling as they run past our house to the hills, "They're coming, it's the militia." and we know it won't be the one some people of our village belong to. And we know the armed men might come to us. My uncle, though living in the city, speaks in the media of our sufferings. We don't run, we have made a hidden shelter, a little room under floor boards, our hiding place, and our bomb shelter. I am fifteen years old but slight and small, have made my own hiding space within the hiding place, a matter of more earth dug out of a corner with nothing but boxes in front of it. We hear the militiamen come in shouting. I hear my grandfather's and grandmother's frightened attempts to calm them and send them away. I hear floor boards being pulled up, people climbing down the ladder, more shouting very close, very loud, very frightening, my sister, my father, my brother's voices cursing them, then noises when I guess they are being forced up the steps. The militia didn't bother to search further, I crouch trembling in my darkness. I wait till the steps and the voices upstairs end. I am thinking hard all that time.

I come up the ladder in a rage. My grandfather's and grandmother's faces are bleeding. They are crying. "They have taken them," they tell me.

"I know." There is nothing we can do. We have no weapons, our militia are away on some other campaign. I stare at my grandparents. "What is it?" they ask me, "What is wrong?" "How did that militia know?" I say. "Who told them about our hiding place? It's new, no one knows, no one outside our family. Who told them?" And I glare at them, not able to decide whether their fear could have made them betray us. After all, who else could have pointed to where we hid? "Not us, you can't think it was us," says my grandfather. "You could even think we'd let our son and our grandson and our granddaughter fall into the hands of those barbarians?" screams my grandmother. They are crying again and telling me over and over they have no idea how the militia knew but they did know and went straight to where they threw the mat aside and then pulled up the floorboards.

But how can I be sure my grandparents tell me all the truth? Round and round in my head goes the puzzle, who else could have found out where we hide? We never hear of nor see any of our family who are taken away again. And all the years I live with my grandparents I never quite trust them, I suspect them, and they know it and every day they cry and plead with me to remember who they are, how they love me and all of us. But I cannot make myself forget I have lost both parents and my brother and sister, so surely it was someone of our family who has told where our secret place is. Sometimes I think of our neighbours, and the boys and girls I've grown up with … could any of them somehow have known about cellar? I don't think so, but how could I ever be sure?

Years later I am in a bus heading for the frontier to escape always being afaid, which was how living in our homeland is, and to get clear of the hunt by the government and other militia for me. A car comes driving the other way and slows by the bus I am in, ready to turn to a side road. I see the driver. She is lit by the sun in front of her, her features are clear. She is my sister. She drives off. And suddenly my tears come and I know my sister must have been the one whose name I'd wanted to know, not my grandparents. Why has she done that? Who has she been working for, who has she been obeying? Not the other militia, not them, surely. The government that hates our people? But why? I don't know anything except that she is secretly alive. I worry at it all the time I am in the bus and while I live in the city in the next-door country and while I am trying to find a way to come here. Had someone made her tell? But she is free, she has a car.

Has she always wanted nothing of what we had been trying to do for our people? Has she hated us, her family? My thoughts jumble and whirl when I am awake and asleep. And my anger grows, and my new puzzle is what to do. How can I do nothing? Just before I leave the country where I have been hiding, I phone my uncle. I tell him I've seen my sister and where and ask what he thinks. And straight away he shouts down the phone, "Traitor, she is the traitor, that ambitious self-serving bitch." And at once I am sorry I've told him. But it is done.

And now I have a new person in our family to hate and to suspect. I hate myself for not forgiving and forgetting, for not allowing my sister to live whatever life she chose. Because now I have sentenced her to death, they will get her, the militia - once my militia - will hunt down a traitor. And I hate myself for the pain of all those years that I caused my grandparents, who I will never now be able to make it up to. And I hate myself for not being able to push aside all these things, these thoughts that whirl constantly in my head, to cut them off, amputate like they were some limb that has got gangrene.

"You see?" I say to my dear one, "you can't trust any of us, we can't trust ourselves."

But what she says is, "You be citizen soon, we get married, and live both at here together."

What is she saying? That is why she says she loves me? I am her passport? Is she ... no no no, my thinking is whirling again, and this, that splinters my mind. I can't choose what to do, what to say to her. I know – and I know I'm weak and stupid and muddle-mixed – sooner or later I'll have to let her choose what we two lovers will do, even if at the same time I'm wondering, Can I trust her? Can I trust myself? And remembering how I'd trusted my sister for years and years, all my life until she passed by for a moment on that road.

She puts her arms around me, she is soft and lovely and she always loves me, I think. She's asking me to look at her hair and see if the new style is nice. But, no, I do not like this style. I wish she would wear it naturally. She has such beautiful hair if she would just let it be. So what should I say? And so she draws me - from my ghosts of betrayed trust and lies that spill blood and cost lives, into a new world of trust with just little deceits, things unsaid. And I should be good at this world shouldn't I.

>Note, two related stories involving the same characters can be found in Desire - stories of lust, longing, love and loss by Eternal Gadd.

BLACK HAT

Grand daughter meets me at the school gate. She is carrying a big plastic bag. She doesn't show me what is inside. As soon as we start to walk she asks, "Can we have an ice-cream on the way home today, grandma?"

"Of course," I tell her. I know what she wants, she wants to talk about something, just her and me, before we get home to her mother. I guess it has something to do with whatever is in her bag.

With our ice-creams we sit on the seat by the bus sign. I hope a bus doesn't come as I wait for her to speak.

"Grandma," she says, "can you hold my ice-cream?"

I hold it as she puts her hand into the plastic bag and very carefully brings out a hat. But it's not a real hat, it's made of something very light. She says nothing, she passes it to me and takes both our ice-creams as I study this hat. "You made it at school?" I ask.

She nods. "For Hat Day. It's paper pieces glued together, and some cardboard for the font piece that sticks out."

"That's the peak," I explain. "I don't know what the word is in English." The hat is not quite round and I feel small lumps on the surface in places, but my grand daughter has made it well. It's black, with a little line of blue around it and below that zigzags of different colours that here and there have run into each other, though the design still looks nice. The top is white with a big black dot in the middle. The peak is black and it's attached with glue and a little cellotape. On my fingers are smudges of paint. "You painted it today?"

"Yes, we made our hats yesterday and the day before, and we put them out in the sun to dry after we painted them this morning."

I'm about to congratulate her when the shape and the main colour catch my attention. I look back at the hat again. Can I be right? Has she tried to make what she remembers of the hats worn by the special police who came to our house in our home country and took away first my son, then my husband and my eldest daughter? How did they know we hated the government? We were always silent. Someone must have reported on us. We saw none of those arrested again. But Anh was so small then.

For a moment I am upset, I want to cry. I want to ask Anh why she has made this hat. Why does she hold onto such hideous memories?

Why has she been silent about them? I turn to her. She watches me, her face is almost white, her little lips press together. Of course, of course, of course, how selfish I am, what a shameful grandmother not to guess that she still after all this time dreams over and over of those days when we were crying and trying to stop the men in the black hats taking the people we loved, and weeping after they had gone into the vans. And she must remember the days and days of worry about when or whether the police would come back for more of us. And how the same things happened to some neighbours and friends. I turn the hat around and around, trying to decide what to say.

At last, "This is a beautiful hat," I tell her.

Suddenly she is smiling hugely. "The teacher likes it too," she says. "Everyone thinks it's the best hat. This afternoon the person who was best behaved in the morning was allowed to wear that hat. Even Sonia, and she talks all the time, tried to be good."

I hug her. We get smears of ice-cream on us, but I don't mind. I decide to tell her, "It reminds me a little of the black hats of the bad men." She looks very serious, even worried. "But you have made this one into a really lovely hat, a hat to tell us to forget those evil men, and to be glad every day that we live in a new country where we are happy and safe and have new friends, and where you have lots of friends at school."

Could her little mind have thought of this, of any of this?

"But will Mum like it?" she is asking.

"No." I am honest with her. "She will see the black and she will remember and she might cry. But we will explain to her this is a hat which everyone in your class admires, it's a hat to celebrate our new lives, it's a hat … " I have an inspiration … "for you to put on the chair by your bed, and it will make your dreams safe. I think your mother will begin little by little to like your hat."

A tear or two squeeze from her eyes. But she is happy. She hides her face in my jacket for a moment as she did when she was smaller.

"Quick," I say getting up, "eat your ice-cream before you have an ice-cream covered hat and bag."

We walk homeward, Anh proudly with her hat not in the bag but on her head. I hold back tears again. If only my husband and son were alive to see this wonderful, brave little daughter and grand child.

Perhaps this hat from school really will help us persuade her mother not to go over and over the sorrows of our past: to remember our family but to keep what must have happened to them far far back in her thoughts, for the sake of Anh.

One of Anh's classmates passes us. She points to the hat and tells the girl with her, "That's the Special Hat I wore today." I give Anh's hand a squeeze.

A STORY FOR FRANK SARGESON

Light from the fluorescent tubes caught at Frank Sargeson's glasses and forehead, and congealed. What had made him look up? I began again to listen.

" ... at anchor, just out there," my grandfather was saying.

"In daylight we could see it from where we're sitting?" asks Sargeson, nodding to where the row of wide, black, curtainless windows leaned towards the sounds of the waves.

"Yes, yes, Arty Yelavich - you remember, the man who built her - can see it from his house a little further along the beachfront but can't go aboard her, can't touch her at all. Day in, day out no one goes near her. All Arty can do is watch the best craft he ever made swing with the tides, getting salt stained and weather marked without once moving from its mooring."

"Why is that?" asked Sargeson.

"I suppose he wants to sell it," said my father. "It would bring him a tidy sum."

"Who," said Sargeson, "Arty Yelavich?"

My grandfather merely drummed exasperated fingers on the threadbare arm of his chair.

"No," said my grandmother, "Sparky Jones, the present owner."

"Sparky Jones and Arty Yelavich," mused Sargeson with a momentary Mona Lisa smile. My grandfather grunted, whether in agreement or aggravation I couldn't decide.

"Arthur Yelavich?" said Sargeson's sister. "Didn't you tell me his wife was so ill that ...?"

But, "This Sparky Jones," Sargeson was already saying, "has possession of Arty Yelavich's boat, right? And he deliberately leaves it anchored in the middle of the bay where everyone can see it? So how did this Sparky Jones manage to get the boat? And why -" Then before anyone could answer, "No - no, tell me this first - why was this the best boat that Arty Yelavich built?"

"He wanted to sail it to Dalmatia," my father explained.

My grandmother heaved to her feet. "I'll fetch the supper, Chook," she told my grandfather.

"Do you want a hand, Chook?" he asked.

"I'll help you," said my aunt, Sargeson's sister.

“No need, Chook," my grandmother told her husband, "it's set out all ready. Thank you," she told my aunt, "but Betty'll do it, she knows where everything is." My mother glanced with annoyance at her mother but rose without a word. She followed cautiously my grandmother's heavy-footed path over a floor layered with worn mats yet showing inches of dark varnished board against each wall. Here and there minute sparkles showed grains of sand swirled from their feet.
“Arty and his three sons," my grandfather was telling Sargeson, "they were going to sail via the Panama."
“It’s a yacht, this boat?"
“A ketch."
"Oh," said Frank.
“Masts fore and aft." Having to explain anything that was self evident irritated my grandfather.
“A sailing boat, then," said Sargeson pacifically.
“No, no," said my grandfather, "he put in an engine too, one he'd made over from the wreck of one of his trucks."
"It must be a large boat."
"Massive," my father said. "I'd never have believed they could get it into the water."
"Wood," said my grandfather into the silence, "that's what he built it of, good sound heart timber, no rubbish anywhere. Made just about every fitting himself. After all he is a builder. I used to give him a hand at times."
"I've done a bit of sandpapering on it myself," said my father. "So's young Jillie here - "
"Yes? Why?" But my cousin continued to sit silently.
My grandfather rasped a roughened hand over his cheek. "Don't know, now you mention it," he said. "I suppose it just seemed there was so much to do, and only the three of them working on it. I've plenty of time on my hands these days."
"It took them years," said my father. "I thought at first it was one of those things people begin and never finish. Every holiday we came here the boat seemed hardly to have changed. But they kept on at it. All through the Summer, too, behind closed doors - "
"Closed ?"
"Oh yes," said my grandmother coming in carrying the tray. My mother followed with the smaller tray of cups and plates. "To keep the nosey

parkers out. You can't have people standing around, not with a boat that size in its cradle. It's dangerous."
"It was to keep out the riff raff," said my grandfather. "Some people round here'd steal anything."
"Even a boat?" suggested Frank.
"It wasn't just a boat," said my grandmother, grunting as she bent to place the tray square on the bamboo table.
"No?"
"The whole family was to go on the voyage, his wife, too."
My grandfather took up the story. "That's why they took so much trouble below decks. It was going to be a long trip, and four or five people living on board."
"The little boy was going, too?" asked my mother.
"Who?" said my aunt. "What little boy?"
"The adopted nephew," my mother told her. "He's only seven or - "
"Ten," said my grandmother. "Yes. Every one of them was to go."
My aunt got up and began to help my mother to hand round the cake and biscuits. It seemed to take them a long time. Every armchair and each of the two sofas was fat and stuffed and of a size to hold my grandparents even though they invariably sat in favourite chairs.
"And they were going to live in Yugoslavia?" Frank prompted.
"Dalmatia," said my grandmother.
"Not live, only visit," my grandfather said. "They couldn't stay there, not with the place being Communist nowadays."
"I think they hoped to sneak in along the coast somewhere," my father put in shaking his head. "Innocents."
"Oh, I should think the Communists would have let them in. What harm could they do visiting their relatives there?" I couldn't resist commenting.
Frank glanced at me. "You think so? I'm always interested to hear what teenagers these days are thinking. I don't meet many."
I tried to think of something else to say to him, something that might help him, something perhaps to put into the mouth of a youthful character in one of his stories. I couldn't think of anything. I looked over at my cousin. She was glancing through a magazine in her lap.
"I suppose it was weekend work," said Sargeson, "building this boat?"
"No fear!" said my grandfather. "Arty couldn't settle to anything else. He was obsessed, you might say. They worked on it, all of the men of the family, practically all the time. And the more ill his wife became,

the more Arty pushed himself. Towards the end I began to wonder if he ever left the craft. I think he must have slept on it. He spent hours finishing off all those fiddly things below decks till everything was exactly right. A beautiful job. I'd never have had the patience myself,"
"Obsessed," echoed Sargeson thoughtfully.
"As if it was his life's goal, his life's - all of their lives' - entire aim," said my father.
My grandmother put down her cup firmly and said, "The point was to get her back in time."
"In time?" my father asked.
My grandfather slurped his tea.
"Before she could die," said my grandmother, "so she could walk the ground of her childhood again."
"And I suppose this boat, this ketch, was as beautiful as he could make it?" said Sargeson.
"Ugly as Sid Holland's mug when he talks about the wharfies," said my father. "And it sits in the water like a barrel."
"But it's a weatherwise craft," said my grandfather. "Arty's a fisherman too." I heard the soft sarcastic grunt my mother gave whenever my grandfather included himself amongst the professional fishermen of the Coast. "He knew what he was doing. It can ride any sea, that boat. Plenty of space below decks, too, considering the size of it. It could take them to Dalmatia perfectly safely. I'd have gone with them, given half a chance."
"He didn't have to paint it that horrible orange," said my mother.
Her father stared at her in surprise. "It can be found easily if it's dismasted or runs into trouble."
"Well," said my mother, "I think it makes the boat a positive eyesore!"
"Even so ... " murmured Sargeson.
"It's the finish," said my grandfather.
"Yes?"
"That's where the craft shows its real class. They put so much time into polishing that decking, and smoothing and painting that hull. I've never seen anything to equal it."
"Ah," said Sargeson.
"Anyway," said my mother, "it proves what I've said all along, they really are wealthy - "
"No," said my grandmother. "The building of the boat took every single thing they had. Their house was put on the market, the building

firm, the electrical shop the older son had, the other boats. When they came back from Dalmatia they wouldn't have had a thing. They'd have had to start all over again."

"I think Mrs Yelavich had some money," said my grandfather. My mother's mouth turned down as it did if he mentioned her name. He pretended not to see, but I was close enough to see the faintest flush where his cheek bones stood out. "But they ran through that during the war years, I think."

"What did he call the boat?" Sargeson wanted to know.

"Homing Pigeon!" My mother said, snorting at the name.

Sargeson merely gestured as if to say, What else?

"He was a pigeon fancier," my grandmother explained.

"Didn't you say that he brought the original breeding pair of birds with him when he first arrived as a young man?" my father asked. "So perhaps he'd had this dream all along."

"And someone stole it?" Sargeson encouraged.

"No!" said my grandfather.

"You said he did," my mother insisted. "You said that Sparky Jones took the boat from him."

"He did not," said my grandmother. "Tell them again, Chook."

"Arty didn't have enough cash to finish it, you see. He couldn't wait for a bank to take its time about it, so he borrowed from the man who always had a bit of spare cash to lend, Sparky Jones. And Sparky waited only a few weeks -"

"I thought it was months," said my mother.

"- till Arty had sold up everything, then came along with the agreement they'd signed and said he needed his money back."

The attorney in Sargeson stirred a moment. "How ... ?"

"Oh," said my grandmother, "he hadn't gone to a lawyer - "

"They were always tight, those Yelavich's," said my mother.

"They'd only got this JP to sign it," said my grandfather.

"And?"

"Arty had no way left to raise the money except by selling his boat."

"And that's it?" asked my aunt. "I thought there was going to be more to the story than that!"

"It's been anchored out there ever since?" Sargeson nodded again at the windows huge as those of a ship's bridge. "For how long?"

"It'll soon be four weeks," said my grandfather.

"So how does Arty Yelavich feel about seeing the boat each day?"

"I reckon," my grandfather answered slowly, "it's like rubbing his nose in his failure."
"He's a nasty piece of work, that Sparky Jones." My grandmother clashed her cup down.
"You had dealings with him once," my mother reminded her father.
"And I burned my fingers and learned my lesson," he said.
My Dad repeated: "Jones'll make a mint of money out of that boat. That's all it means to him."
"What's Arty doing now?" asked Sargeson.
"He has to rent his own property," said my grandfather. "He has to go into the city and work on one of those trawler fishing boats."
"He's really grieved." My grandmother dabbed at her eyes. "He's a broken man, a bitter man."
"So it was Sparky Jones who launched the boat in the end?"
My grandparents nodded at Sargeson's guess.
"Arthur Yelavich deserves to have lost it," said my mother. "It was a ridiculous thing to do. I don't believe they'd have got half way round the world in that bit of a boat whatever you say. It was just a selfish fantasy, and it's cost them everything they had. I've no time for that sort of thing." She glared at her father. He looked away, his eyes seeming to move without seeing over this largest room of the seaside bach he'd spent his retirement money on.
"No, no, no," murmured my grandfather, "you're wrong, it meant everything to them."
"Her, too," said my grandmother, "it was what they all wanted."
"Well, I don't think," said Sargeson, "that Arty will put up with someone destroying all that faith and hope and work, and in that way, too!"
"So what do you think he'll do?" challenged my grandfather.
My grandmother, too, glanced keenly at Sargeson. In the hard white light they looked as if carved almost identically from slabs of wood.
"I don't know," said Sargeson. My grandparents stared at him still.
"He'll find something, that's certain," Sargeson went on. "The story hasn't come to an end yet. And there are other things in it that intrigue me - that name, for instance, Sparky Jones ... mmmm." He shrugged.
"All I'm sure of is that something will happen, and very soon. Well," he bent, groping under his chair for his little rucksack or whatever it was.
"I'll miss the last bus if I don't go now."

At the window a brilliance flared, dimming the blaze of the fluorescent tubes. A muffled thump followed. My cousin jumped up onto the settee in front of the windows. "Turn off the light!" she shouted. "It's that boat you keep talking about!"
"By Jove, she's right," said my father. "Norris, do you remember that fire at the Bible Class camp in - ?"
"Someone had better do something," cut in my mother as she always did when they started talking of things shared before she'd known them.
My grandfather sat rasping his cheek and laughing quietly, making little ss-ss sounds. He said admiringly to Sargeson, "Sparky! Sparky Jones! You'd guessed what was going to happen, hadn't you?"
"Don't you dare take any credit!" said his sister to Sargeson. "You hadn't any more idea than the rest of us what would happen!"
Sargeson said nothing, slipped the strap of his bag over his shoulder.
"Come on," urged my cousin, "we'd better get down there to see what's happening." She ran out of the room.
"Plenty of other people will have seen it by now," said my grandmother placidly peering with her short-sighted eyes. "I hope no one was hurt."
"I'll go down to the beach and see if a hand's needed," my father said.
"Can we drive you home?" suggested my mother to Sargeson.
"No, I prefer the bus," he said. He nodded around. "Good-bye, then. It's been interesting."
My grandfather was still laughing. "You're a proper caution," he told Sargeson as he led him into the passageway, "especially as I hadn't told you yet how Sparky re-named the boat, Flint, after this place in Wales."
"After his heart," my grandmother called after them.
"Richard the Second," muttered Sargeson.
"That's it, that's the one," said my grandfather. "A *quietus*, eh?" I looked at him in surprise. "But there's one more thing - Sparky was Mrs Yelavich's first husband! Years ago, before we'd moved here."
Sargeson smiled. "You, too - both of you - knew all along what Arty might do!" He laughed. "I'd have been quite proud to have written that story!"
My grandfather said so quietly that I could barely hear, "All I knew for a fact was that when a man marries again there's bound to be hurt and trouble, you know?" His eyes slid towards my mother and away again as he rubbed his chin, eyes on Sargeson.

But, "See you some time again, Os," was all Sargeson said as he went down the creaking wooden steps, along the path and out of the half-circle of light.

THE NIHILIST

There isn't really much of a story to tell. Besides, my grandfather was the only one who knew exactly what happened, and as you know, he's been dead years. I think he used to feel it was a bit of a joke when he told me that he'd been the last Nihilist in the world, and the only kiwi Nihilist there'd ever been, and would swear me to share that fact with no one else. I was quite young then. A Nihilist? Assassins, I suppose, who aim to destroy people like autocratic Kings, aristocrats, Prime Ministers and the offices they hold. The terrorists of the day, yes. I think he must have picked up the idea when he was in Europe with his parents, and they got to know some Russians. He always had a word or two of Russian to show off. This of course was before Lenin's revolution.

A very idealistic man he was, and immensely angry at some of the things he saw. Ironically, no matter how greatly he loathed ruthless power as a Nihilist, as a man he couldn't bear the thought of bloodshed let alone calculatedly planning to kill or maim anyone. And equally he loathed the notion of destroying any building or monument that was old or beautiful no matter what it was and whether what they memorialized appalled him.

Do you remember the *Weekly News* and the *Freelance*? Pink covered magazines they were, newspaper size newsprint pages but some glossier ones as well for black and white photos. No? Too young? Anyway, those are what he chose to destroy as representing to him, I imagine, worthless ideas and exaltation of worthless people he couldn't so much as try to blot out but whose images he could literally blacken. Not whole print runs, he had no way to do that, just those copies of the magazines which arrived at the city where he lived. He must have known how pointless it was, how unlikely it was that the publishers would get sufficiently scared or annoyed to close down the magazines. But he longed to at least make some sort of a gesture, naïve or not, futile or not.

I'm not sure what his job was, in some sort of an office in the part of the city handy to the railway station. Possibly that's what gave him the idea for his Nihilist campaign.

The magazines would be unloaded from the goods wagon very early in the morning, dumped on the platform in roped-up bundles to be collected by the distribution agent. My grandfather clearly had discovered a brief time when no one was in charge of the bundles, giving him time to set them on fire. Maybe he used a primitive form of the Molotov cocktail, but I think he must have been pretty hopeless as a bomb maker. In all the old newspapers I've looked at no report mentions more than that some of the bundles of magazines were extensively charred. I guess that tightly packed magazines of newsprint aren't the easiest items to burn. The whole affair hardly flared in the papers, though I've no doubt that the publishers and the subscribers were irritated and got onto the police.

But he'd certainly a skill in concealment because there's no hint that anyone suspected him or even thought of him as a feasible suspect.

His real problem was that the police eventually chose as prime suspects his brother, the station master, and the magazines' distribution agent, a good family friend. Both of them were, it seems, impeccably conventional and most unlikely to connive at any such deeds, but the police must have been desperate to accuse someone. This was the great crisis of my grandfather's life as an activist: how to keep his own role hidden and thus his Nihilistic programme potentially revivable, but to utterly remove suspicion from his brother and friend.

His solution was breathtaking in its contempt for ordinary logic let alone scientific fact. But he'd rightly guessed that any proposal banal enough for a busy public person to grasp in an instant – and with some kind of literary reference appended – could claim credibility. He wrote a letter to the city newspaper suggesting that the cause of the problem was … spontaneous combustion caused by the printers using ink that ignited after prolonged friction in the railway wagon. He reminded that no less a person than Mr Charles Dickens had depicted the spontaneous combustion of a person in one of his novels, and that improbable or not as that event might have been, there were solid grounds for believing spontaneous combustion to be the case for the bundles of *Weekly Newses* and *Freelances*. Of course he offered in his letter none of those supposed grounds. But the suggestion was taken up at once by the Mayor, the magazine publishers (though not the annoyed printers), and the detectives. Some changes were made, I don't know what, to make sure it didn't happen again. His brother and friend were immensely grateful to him and showered even me too with an overflow of kindness for the rest of their lives.

Of course that was the end of his Nihilism campaign, he couldn't very well go ahead and disprove his own combustive theory and set alight the now especially non-spontaneous-combustible packaged magazine bundles. Right to the last he'd wheeze with laughter at how eager folk had been to take up his absurd suggestion. And the best of the joke for him was that as a result of that triumph, he was waited on – as they said in those days – by many people and urged to stand for the Council, was duly elected and spent many contented years opposing all manner of suggestions for monuments to and honours for wealthy citizens, gaining a reputation for commonsense and integrity.

Did my grandmother ever guess what he'd been up to? You know, I've a notion she did. I base that only on a slide of her eye if she heard me as an adult give the slightest hint at the matter. She said nothing to anyone, ever, least of all grandfather. A loyal wife? An amused one? She was, after all, an avid reader of her weekly *Freelance.* And in an issue we still retain in the family, there was my grandfather's mustachio'd photo as the astute solver of the conundrum of the incendiary magazines.

COUSIN AURORA'S CONCERT PERFORMANCE

Dad's turning up the radio, shouting for Mum to come. It's that cousin again. An interview this time, she and some other woman blahing away about how marvelous she is and of course wonderful cousin Aurora's agreeing all along the line. Dad doesn't waste time calling me. Look, all she does is play the piano and all by herself, not even with a band let alone a singer. If you ever try to talk to her about anything interesting, she loses interest straight away and she's likely to walk off while you're talking. She's no idea where the hot spots are in the places she visits, or if the girls are cool, or what the latest stuff is. She says things like, "I go to play, that's my work, I have to practice, I've no time to horse about." Yeah yeah. And if I talk about what I'm doing, her eyes glaze real fast. You'd think she could show interest in the places I've been. She's not the only one who travels, and I don't have to get inside a jet. She never asks what I'm doing in the judo champs.

There's worse. She's back from Aussie for her Kiwiland Concert Tour (her idea of a grab-the-people title). And tonight we're all going to this hall to listen, no excuses. Oh man, maybe two, three hours. Aurora for sure'll play on and on and on and there's nothing for it but let your brain zone out.

But hey, I'm getting an idea, right out of the blue. I'm good at something else, too, not just the judo stuff. Gadgets, I can tinker with them, eh. What slips me the idea is Mum and Dad going over with her the things Aurora wants to play and Mum saying "Oh no, don't start with that one, it's quite pretentious, the composer was frankly, dear, a show-off." But Aurora's going to have it. Well of course, guess who's the show-off of the hour?

So, yep, it's real easy to action what I've got in mind. We're in the hall and I'm real helpful. There aren't even any people here yet, that's how early we are. I take her favourite cushion for her piano stool on stage. And I insert this neat little gizmo under one of the piano wires. Easy as.

A bit later we're filing in, sitting down – close to the front, you betcha – and I'm waiting and I'm not smirking, have this so bored face on. And away she starts, hands up high then diving them down, head going tick tock, neck rigid, all clear as daylight in her short sleeve gown. I'm tense and waiting… and yep, soon as a finger's on that certain key out comes the sound like someone's blowing a raspberry. She goes right on, nothing's showing on her face. I have to admit she's a pro up there on a stage. But there's a bit of a snigger and Mum and Dad sit up as if they've been stung.

The noise comes again, there're sniggers and a chuckle or two. But hey, she's starting to sway, make her arms fly up, crash down, her head's going crazy this side and that, she's hamming it up, she's pausing a nano-sec before each raspberry. Heaps of the audience laughing and, man, she's a comedy turn with this show-off piece. And it's just a few like Mum and Dad are frowning. The piece ends and Aurora's bouncing up, taking a crazy bow, then shoves her hand inside the grand, takes out the gizmo, shows it, puts it on the floor beside her. And just about everyone's clapping.

It's straight playing the rest of the way. It's the final encore – yeah, unbelievable, they can't get enough of her plunk plunk plunk – she's fitting my gizmo back and clowning up and down the keys in another tune. And this is fine too with most of these in the hall.

After she talks to people who crowd up to meet her (she never shakes a hand). We go off to a late night feed. I tuck in, I can tell you I'm starving. And she's saying nothing to me, not giving so much as a look and I'm thinking, Score one for her, she's never let on to anyone if she was anyway thrown by my gizmo. Could be, you know, she hasn't figured I'd planted the thing.

Come morning Mum drives her to the 'plane for another town and that's that.

My mobile goes at school, and I look at it under cover of the table: *not funny brad not funny don't u try anything on me again when im performing thats my living you idiot*

Have to get the mobile into my pocket in a hurry when the teacher comes round. So ok she's put the finger on me and she's mad. That'll pass, and see if I care if it doesn't. But my mobile goes every minute with that identical message. No one else gets in a single text. How can she do that? It's impossible, and anyway where's she get the know-how? Might as well have a hunk of plastic parked in my pocket. My social life's ruined. How'm I supposed to get in touch with the new girl from Macau? Go up to her and say, "Hey, Suzie, you're hot." What'd she think I was? An ape man? Cloud music, latest apps, voice control,

direct Facebook links, anything you think - her mobile's got it and more.
It's three days and I'm out of the loop, I only know whatever people bother to tell. That Aurora! Talk about … what's the word? … oh yeah, vindictive. What a maxi sulk she's throwing!
Saturday, and a new message (just as well I keep on checking, eh): *remember keep out of my career*, and I'm back in touch. I'm mad at her, sure, but hey, I have to admit it, Aurora's got smarts, man, she's not a piano thumper only … even if she's no idea how anyone lives.
If she comes back again this way, I'm out of here before her recital … yeah, and I guess she'll go with that.
Oh, it's Suzie on the mobile. Hey, man, I'm getting pix … and video … oh no - she's clattering away at scales on a fat piano - plunk plunk! No way. Not her too. How to get out of this fast?

MY FIRST JOB

"Let your little David come down to my place each Saturday at 10 o'clock - I've got a nice little job for him," said Mrs H to our mum. "I'll give him truppence."
"Do I have to," I asked our mum - once Mrs H was gone.
She smiled patiently at me. "We need the money she said."
Yes, I knew that. But I thought my first real paying job might be a little more - well, I don't know, something more dignified, more grown up.
But I went all the way down the hill to Mrs H's place. The job was to be lifted up by the tall lady on to her kitchen table, then "close your eyes and don't open them till I tell you."
Then came the task of doing up her corset from the back, then the long job of 'hooking and eyeing' her long black dress, all from behind. There seemed hundreds of them and too many eyes and not enough hooks to match. And it was a very long dress, a frilly one, and black, that reached to the ground. And the lady was very tall and buxom to boot.
She was not an easy boss - "too tight" or "too loose" or "don't fidget" or "too slow."
But by the end I became pretty good at the job and was thinking of asking for a rise in wages, for I felt ashamed at doing such a menial task. By now, with it almost done, and she sneaking peaks of herself in the mirror and evidently liking what she saw, she was in a genial mood.
I had hardly finished when she said "and how old are you my little man."
"Nine," I said. I could feel her stiffen beneath my fingers.
"Nine!" she shouted. "Nine! You're nothing but a cheat, you ought to be ashamed of yourself. I thought by the size of you, you were only five. Get out, go on, get out or I'll call the police."
I got out fast alright and fled home in tears to mum - minus the truppence.
"Well that didn't go so well, did it," mum said.
I just stood there, cheeks flaming. Not at all how I had wanted my first bit of real work to go.
At least the next one couldn't be as bad, whenever the next opportunity came.
And at least it wouldn't be that awful Mrs H as employer.

Shows what I knew.
Because Mrs H must have got over the shock, for some weeks later she sent for me again. Just one job - an easy one - for sixpence this time.
I refused to go, but mum said "she's a good customer - you'll have to go."
I went - very slowly.
"Ah! My big man," said Mrs Hunt. I examined her face. Not a hint of irony. Just the normal self conceited smugness.
She handed me a huge axe. "Come with me," she said. We walked to the back of the large garden and she introduced me to a real giant of birds. A huge creature that gazed at me and stretched its long neck
"I just want you to chop its head off - it's our Christmas dinner," said Mrs H. "Come to the front when you've finished and bring me the axe back and I'll pay you sixpence."
She fled away pretty fast while I eyed the goose - or was it a black swan? The bird eyed me for a while.
I gulped. Well, this was certainly more grown up as a job.
I stood there, this great lumping axe in hand eyeing that bird and the beast eyeing me back. Then it stretched again its long neck, opened its mouth, and hissing came towards me.
For a moment I stood petrified, then with a loud yell, I dropped the axe and fled - minus the sixpence.
Grown up jobs could wait till I was grown up.

BROTHER

I opened the door. A young guy about my age was standing there, smiling. He stared, for an instant looking at me as a man looks at a woman, and then – his smile growing huger – as if he waited for some response.

"Yes?" I asked.

"You don't recognise me?" he asked. "Dane?"

"Dane?" I stared back at him, confused. What was he saying? Why did he keep watching like that? I began to feel a little apprehensive of this man.

His smile widened further. He spread his arms. "Use your eyes, girl."

Surprised, I looked straight into his face. Something – there was something there, but … He was laughing. "Elaine –" He knew my name "- it's me, your long lost kid brother. I'm Dane."

"My brother!"

His hug carried me back into the room. We clung to each other, laughing, crying. And the questions came and came: "How are mum and dad?" "How's aunty Tess and uncle Pat?" "Are they still living in the old place? Did they ever talk about me, Dane?" "How come you have this big flash place eh?" "Did they ever say why I was sent to aunty Tess to be brought up?" "You've got a boyfriend, girl?" "What are you doing in the city?" "Do you keep in touch with any of the family?" "How did you know where I was?"

We stopped and grinned at one another. We were like little kids, talking and talking without stopping for a reply. But it didn't seem to matter. There'd be time for answers. I noticed a bag he'd dropped in a corner.

"So where are you staying?" I asked him, feeling I already knew the brother I'd never met well enough to guess at what he'd say. His eyes laughed at me again.

"Oh," he said. "Where ever I can find a place." "You're lucky," I told him. "This place has two bedrooms." And his eyes really lit when I said, "That one can be yours." "Eh!" he said, and slung his bag in through the door. "What'll we do tonight to celebrate, Sis?"

"Take you to the pub to show you off to my mates, of course. And tomorrow night you'll meet Don." "Don?" "We're going to get married," I explained. "That's why I've got a place this size, see,

waiting for us." "You share?" "No," I said. He shook his head as if disbelievingly.
We enjoyed ourselves. He told the people at each new place we went, "And I never even knew I had this gorgeous sister!" Everyone liked him. "Don't you go keeping him to yourself," they kept saying to me. "Nah, Elaine and me, we've got a lot of catching up to do," he'd say to them when they offered to take him out and show him the sights.
It was late when we made for home, there were no buses. We went arm in arm, "I'd never dare to walk this way alone," I said. "Ah, girl, you've just never had a bro to look after you before."
Next morning he put his head in the bedroom door and said, "Up! I've made you your breakfast." I staggered out, I was still sleepy. I stared around. "Hey, why did you put the weetbix up there? That's only to divide the kitchen from the dining room." He shrugged. I tried not to laugh. He started smiling too. "Aw," he said, "you know what sort of a place I'm used to, Sis." "No," I said, "I can't remember it at all." He got up and hugged me, "Come on girl, forget that old stuff. We're together now, eh?"
The phone went. Don said, "What's going on?" "Nothing," I said, "why?" "It's your voice, you sound like you're having an early morning party or something." "No," I said, "no, I'm only happy. Don, my brother that I've never met before is here. Come round, now, I want you to meet him." "Yeah?" he said. "Great. I can't though, I've got to get to the Tech early, remember?" "Give it a miss," I urged. "Can't," he said, "it's too close to exams. And this evening –" "Hold on, then, I'll put Dane on the line."
"Dane?" I asked when he put down the phone. He was frowning slightly. "He's the guy who's going to marry you?" "Yep. And?" He did his shrug. "He's not coming round to see you tonight after all." "No." He suddenly grinned. "Then it's up to me to make sure you have a good time tonight. So where'd you want to go?"
When Don did come around, he told Dane, "I think I know a place where you can stay." "I'm ok here, thanks," Dane told him. "It's a lot cheaper," said Don. "No problem," said Dane. "I've been at the Works the whole season." "The works?" Even I knew that one: "The Freezing Works," I explained. "Save your money," Dane said to him. "While I'm here I'll pay the rent." "Half," I reminded. "The rent," said Dane. "No –" began Don. "Now where to tonight?" Dane asked us.

"That new night club?" I suggested. "It's their opening night." "The club it is," said Dane. "How about we make it the pub tonight?" said Don. "I've got exams tomorrow. Those places go on too late." "You leave early, then," said Dane. Don's eyes flashed
a moment. I said quickly, "No, the club can wait." "You're sure?" Dane wanted to know. "Sure," I said.

But Dane got dressed up as if we were going to the club opening anyway. Everyone at the pub kept glancing at him and then at us in our ordinary gear. I had to smile. "What's he want to wear all that stuff for to come here?" said Don when Dane was getting us a round. I told him, "I think it's his idea of having a laugh on me for not getting to that club." "What?" "Relax," I said. "I think it really is quite funny." Don grunted. "All right," he said, "the club tomorrow. But you make sure you give us a good feed before we go ok? They rip you off, those places." "Here you go," said Dane putting down some tall cold glasses with drops like tears sliding down their sides. "They reckon this is the best drink the house serves." Don stared, startled. "Drink up, Don boy," said Dane, "enjoy!"

The next morning Dane suddenly said, "Elaine, I hear there's some great beaches out on the coast." "That's right, we can go this Saturday." "No," he said, "look at that weather out there, it's too good to waste. Take the day off work, why don't you?"

I said, "I can't. I mean, we're saving and –" "A day?" he looked a me, hurt. "One day?" "Oh I suppose so," I agreed at last. "All right!" he said. "That's my sister!"

We went by bus We swam, and lazed on sun-hot sand all day. "I guess I'd better start looking for a place of my own," he said. "What for?" I asked. "I don't want to crowd you and Don," he said. "How could you? You're my brother. We've still got a lot of years to catch up on. I don't want you to move out." And as I said it I realised how true it was that I didn't want to lose again the brother I'd never seen.

Almost as if to follow on from my thoughts he murmured, though maybe more to himself than me, "If we were at home we could be swimming with our mates in our own private bend of the river without having had to buy swim suits so that we could sit in front of a toilet block with a bunch of strangers."

A few days later a friend sat next to me on the bus to work. "Saw you at the pub last night," she said. "You're in luck all right." "Oh?" "Having *two* such good looking guys after you." I laughed. "No?" I

explained. "The one you haven't seen before isn't a boy friend, he's my brother, Dane." "Really?"
The astonishment in her face stayed in my mind all day. What had she meant? Oh, I knew what she'd meant. Why had she thought that? How could she have made that mistake?
When I reach home Dane handed me a little package. It was a bracelet, gold. "Thought it'd look good on you," he said. "Wear it when we go out tonight, Elaine." When Don noticed it he glanced away, said nothing. He hardly said anything to me that night. I stared down at my hand uneasily. I saw how the band of the ring he'd given me and the bracelet seemed to gleam with exactly the same colour of gold.
Dane kissed me goodnight as he sometimes did. I want to bed, and lay awake going over and over words and events. I recalled everything Dane had ever said to me. I tried to sense again the feel of his lips, to assess what that could tell me. I tried to decide if the gift of the gold bracelet should be hinting things to me, what his insisting I took the day off work might mean, and those musings of his at the beach. I thought of Don's reactions to Dane and to all that Dane had done and said. But where was there anything to tell me clearly what I was to Dane?
"Hey!" he said in alarm as soon as he saw me next morning. "You're sick." "No," I said. "I'm alright." "Get right back to bed, you can't go to work like this." "I'm all right!" "You can hardly walk straight. And you've got a temperature." "Leave me alone!" He simply picked me up, dropped me back on my bed. "If aunty Tess was anything like mum she'd never let you go to work looking like that, girl. I'll get some hot tea, that's what mum'd do." "I don't want it," I said. "Get your nightie back on," Dane said. "Or do I have to do it for you?" "Get out!" I said.
A dark weight pressed my head down upon my raised knees. Men hardly ever acted like this, not even brothers. I was sure of it.
He looked in. "I'm going to the chemist for some aspirin for you," he said. "Won't be long."
When you were sick men were just impatient for you to get well again, even the ones in the family. They'd hardly do anything for you unless you were actually too ill to move a finger. And I wasn't really sick.
No, he didn't want to be like a brother to me at all. That girl was right. She'd seen the truth.

What could I do? I felt something jabbing into my palm. I looked down. I'd worked the ring and bracelet of. I laid them aside on the dressing table. Don – I should go and talk with him. I could not make myself get off the bed. What was wrong with me?

He'd seemed exactly right for me when I'd met him. But having Dane around had made me look at Don almost as though meeting him again. I could see how much he'd focussed both our lives on that determination of his to do well. How many simple ordinary good times had Don and I missed out on over the months?

I switched my mind from those thoughts. I ought to go to him. Yet I didn't want to talk about Dane with him. I couldn't.

Soon Dane would be back. What would happen then? I remembered his strong arms carrying me back to bed, the arms that seemed to have been around me so often these past days. And the eyes that seemed to light when he looked at me, just like that first time he saw me. And his li-. I groaned aloud. What was I wanting? What feelings were these? What was he doing to me?

I thought I heard steps on the path outside. I jumped from the bed, stripped the nightdress off, pulled on levis and a shirt, I had no time for more. I couldn't worry about the rest of my things.

I opened the window, climbed quietly out.

"I'm back."

I ran out the gate. "Elaine?"

I rushed across the street between cars. Someone would lend me the money for the bus home. Was there any place left for me to go except to aunty Tess and uncle Pat? Was there anything else I could do?

THE LADY MACBETH ESSAY

"Yes, Miss, I'm starting right now."
Can't she leave me alone? Why keep watching me? All right, all right, I'll turn my mind to it, try to put something down, get her stare off me. What?
Lady Macbeth was a real help at the start to her husband. But in the end night after night she was sleep-walking getting no rest, always acting out again those same terrible things .... she'd been trying so hard never to remember all day long. Except they'd always be waiting to come pouncing out, clinging at her thoughts.
In the end she spent every night as if she was trying to find a door to get away from her memories. And those two people watching, listening, were useless, did nothing to help.
Yet they believed what they heard. Even my mother wouldn't believe me. "Stop going on about it," she'd said, "stop fibbing. What could you know about things like that, a girl like you?"
Even when my tears oozed she couldn't take me seriously, kept wanting to know what was truly the matter with me. *And the man who'd said he loved her was never there to help her.*
"He's my mate," Dad told me, "he's OK, he wouldn't do a thing like that, you're being spiteful, you just don't like having someone else in the house to make more work for you. Now shut it, Tanya, I'm sick of it."
So who could I tell who'd keep quiet, who wouldn't look down on me? *She'd been brave, too, this Lady. She'd taken the daggers, she'd made the whole assassination go to her plan.* Me, I couldn't think what to do, what to say to him, how to push him away. I was feeble, was weak, I'd lie there, still, silent, taking it. I hated and hated myself.
Maybe I deserved it. Because why pick on me? What did he see that told him he could do it? Was it that sometimes, just occasionally, in spite of everything, my body seemed to say "Yes"? It was learning things I didn't want to have to learn every night, all that long time. And scared, I was so scared .... *"Bring forth"* ... And every day pretending I wasn't sick with shame. And knowing he didn't care about me. Hardly spoke, ever. *"A little water clears us of this deed. .. "* Lies! She was telling herself lies.

She took that dagger to herself in the end, she had the guts to. And no more thinking. No more dreams. No more worrying. No feeling filthy all the time. Quiet, perfect oblivion ....

Don't think, Miss with your red hair like you say this Lady Macbeth had, you guess what I'm thinking about. Or could suspect what I've got here in my pocket.

It'd be easy to do it, right now, get up, ask to go to the loo and .... And why not? Why not do as Lady Macbeth did? Tonight he'll be back, who knows for how long this time. Will it start up again this year? All over again I'll be like the characters in this play who haven't got so much as a name, are used, just used.

"Ouch!" You could cut yourself on the edge of these foil strips. *"Who'd have thought the old man to have had so much blood in him?'*

Mum and Dad will know for sure when they learn what I've done that I was always telling the truth.

Miss, I've decided, I won't go through those sorts of nights again. I'm going to get up, walk out, gulp down these little things. I'm going .... now!

Who's outside the classroom? I'll wait.

What? "No, I'm all right, Miss." See? I'm putting my head down, getting back to work. For a few minutes more. Till.... What's Lady Macbeth saying?

" You do unbend your noble strength to think so brain sickly of things .... " She was the one that had all the noble strength. In the end there was none left for herself? While me ....

Still watching me, teacher lady, still frowning?

Well.... could I jam the bed across the door? Tell him out loud in front of the family, "Not this year, man, you'll have to slap me around first? "

Or. .. or ... ? Come on, come on, I'm not brain sickly!

I'll have something worked out. By the end of today. Sure to!

One more minute for this essay? So OK.

Me, I think she was a brave woman, terrible but brave. It was just that she was old, she was so exhausted with getting her husband out of tough places that her strength gave out, she could think of only one way to make it all come to its end.

There you are, Miss, brief - but good! And true! Tonight? I'll screw my courage to the sticking point! And I'll not fail!

A HOUSE OF US

Bloody honky bitch!
"I'm sorry, Mr Oteenee -"
Shit! "Otene!"
"- but your unemployment benefit will not start for another three days. If you are in need of cash for that period, you may fill in this application form."
Not me, not another bloody form!
"Oh, and we're still awaiting confirmation from your last employer are you sure ... "
That sweating bastard! Why the hell did I have to piss around here waiting for that punk's say so? Stuff the bloody lot of them. I pushed my way out and down the steps. Who the hell did those stuck-up bastards up there think they were anyway?
Screeching dinned right in my ear. They thought I'm some kind of flea to hop around their bloody cars?
Couldn't even get to the pub, damn bus cleaned out my dough. So I walked all that way back home. Jeez, by the time I got there I was a walking waterfall of sweat. And yep, there they all were, might've guessed it, knocking back the booze like tomorrow'd been scratched. Paul, Tina, Suzie, the dole gang. And Eddie, eyes half closed because he was on the night shift. And Waaka, used to go to University, scrub-cutting now.
"I hope you bloody brought some of your own booze," I told them. And damn, look, there was that skinny kid sister of mine, wagging high school again and smoking like she'd got hold of the last butt in the world, sitting on the floor making like she was real grown up. "What the hell you -"
Just as if opening my mouth was his signal, in roared Billy Marsters. He was hardly in the door when he was yelling at us. "Hey, hey, listen to this, I got a cool idea!" He was going to tell us all about it too, like it or not, I could see that. Oh boy, I cleared a couple of them off the sofa and lay down, put a row of cans on my gut so's not to give the thirst a chance. "All right, all right," I told him, "get it off your chest before your brains burn out."

"Listen," he said, "I just been down the creek, and see there's this whole stack of branches and stuff and man, you wouldn't believe it, it was a hut, the most hakari hut - "

"Yeah, that's where those street kids have built them a hut," said my smart-arse sister.

"Shuddup," I told her.

"Yeah? Well, look, just suddenly there I was remembering, seeing it clear as that heap of sticks, this old-time Maori village, you know, the one we saw on that school trip up north?" And he told us, man did he tell us. You know what his idea was all about? You just wouldn't believe it. All about this old-time wharemoe - you know, there's just these two walls of upright pongas jammed close together, about a metre apart, and the gap between 'em stuffed tight with bracken and stuff. And the roof beam about ten foot high and the roof made of strips of manuka bark running from one side up over the roof beam and down the other side, strip after strip till the roof was real thick and watertight. And against the walls you heaped dirt till only a few inches of wall showed. The whole thing's big enough for a couple of rugby teams to sit down inside. Man, he was that excited he was practically foaming. And then came the crunch - I'd been waiting for it. "See, we could build one, a wharemoe for us."

True! That's just what he said!

"Just us, show 'em all. We can make a place for us."

Jesus! It made my tongue so dry just to think of anybody doing it, I had to swallow a couple of cans straight off.

"You mean you want us to build one of those things?" Paul's eyes stuck out like baseballs.

"Sure, we could do it together, just easy," said Billy. Then they started in.

"Oh sure, real easy!"

"What use?"

"Who the hell wants it?"

"Stuff all that hard work, turkey!"

"No way you get me out there!"

"You got a history book in place of a brain, boy?"

Billy was staring round at us looking real sad and surprised. "Oh come on ..." he said. You could see the fire in his eyes dying out bit by bit. Poor guy.

I might've been feeling mad at those fullas from this morning, but no way I was going out to sweat over no old house just to show them or anyone. Who the hell'd care a stuff if I did?

Waaka stirred. Well, well, what was the big brain going to come out with? "Could be done," he said.

Far out!

"Ho, listen to the man," said Suzie.

"No, wait, it has been done. Lots of times. But always for the tourists or the museum or something. Never for the Maori, never to use."

"So?"

"Just there're still old fullas around the place know about that kind of stuff."

I felt tired. The springs growled as I wriggled back further. "Who cares?" I told him.

"Tell you what," Billy's girl, Tina, suddenly said. "All of us been saying to Billy, 'How to do it?' See? No one's turned the idea down flat yet - no, not really. Look, we're still sitting here talking about it, aren't we?" Loyal girl, that one.

And suddenly my bony sister Girlie sat up and said, "Know what? I reckon all yous are too ashamed to say it out loud that even street kids can build them a place - but you couldn't."

"You give me a pain," I told her. "Piss off to school. Look, who needs all this old-time stuff?"

"No, listen, maybe just us really could do it," said Waaka, "and really show we've got our own feet we can stand on."

"Oh sure," said Paul.

"But that's exactly it," said Billy. You could see the keenness roaring up his veins like a dragster. "To show we're sick of being pushed around, hired, fired, crapped on, the lot, just to suit them. We show all those out there we got things we can do, our own things."

"Yeah," said Tina, talking slowly like she was digging the words up from somewhere, "that kind of place could be ok, too. Billy says to use all this old-time Maori stuff, eh. But look, on this floor we got these island mats, these cushions - "

"Hey!" Waaka looked like he was about to do the haka. "Old-time know-how, modern know-how. It'd be a winner! You could really live in that!"

"You do it," said Paul, "too much slog all that."

I could see the picture in my mind while they kept on. Be like a sort of a permanent club house. For a screwy idea it could be all right too. All of us there together. No one to bug us. But, boy, if you had to build it first! No prefab wharemoes! Get the land, get the stuff - oh man. No way!
"Go the whole way," said Paul sarcastically, "grow your own *kai*."
"Doubt it," said Suzie.
"Barter."
"Huh?" We all stared at Waaka.
"Could do it," he said. "make things, do odd jobs, get food and stuff back in return. No money."
"Well that might work," said Eddie. "Might."
"Hey, you mean -" it was Girlie.
"Thought I told you to bugger off to school," I yelled at her. This was crazy. They'd be taking this seriously next. Girlie took no notice.
"You mean yous really going to do Billy's idea?" She looked lit up. One crazy kid!
"Don't be stupid," said someone.
But, "We could do it," Waaka said at last.
I groaned. "Good," I told him. "I volunteer" - I put a can up my mouth "- to sit and watch that is," I mumbled to myself.
"Yeah, and what if I can get some university mates to help do the really hard slog?" he said.
Pity in a way that it couldn't work. I can dream, too, you know. Too bad, though. "Then let them," I said. I'd had a gutsful of their talk. I turned over and went to sleep.
When I woke up I got one hell of a shock. There was just Billy left and, "Hey," he said, "thanks."
"Huh?"
"I reckon it was you persuaded them - oh and those mates of Waaka's promising to bring us a feed of mussels and kina to start us all off."
I got a sudden bad suspicion. "Tell me what's going on."
"Yes, man, we're doing it. True!"
Ohno!
"See, Waaka rang up and fixed up those guys to help. Be like an experiment to them. They're going to do the hassle - fix about a site, get stuff, get some old guy to advise, all that. Dig, even."
"Sure," I said, "and they get to have the place in the end."

"Not to worry," he said grinning, "they're too chicken to try living in a place like that. But boy, you were the one who really surprised our own mates into agreeing to it."

What had I said to bring all that on? Man! My muscles ached at the thoughts. Someone must have been stoned!

So that's how come I got to go running all round the place in this guy's truck, picking stuff up, going into the bush. And when at last it was all piled out on the bit of land up the creek that the Council let us use, we just looked at it.

Jeez! Bracken, kanuka branches, pongas, poles. You never saw anything like it.

Suzie kicked a heap of bracken. "This is bloody stupid," she said.

"I got it," I said, "it's Guy Fawkes. We just got the month wrong."

"That's our free board and lodging," said Waaka.

"Doubt it," said Suzie.

"Aw come on, I'm for home," said Paul. "You want to play old Maoris, you go ahead. But not me. This is far as I go."

"Yeah, I'm not living in no moa's nest," said Suzie.

"You lot just too bloody hoha to try anything!" It was that damned Girlie screeching at us, "too bloody mangere!"

I'd had it with that Girlie. "Get the hell out of it," I roared at her. "What you doing here anyways? Get out of it and get to school, you hear?" I was going to give her a crack to send her on her way.

"Hold it," said Eddie.

"Get lost, poaka," she yelled at me. "I reckon Billy's idea's a neat one."

"Oooooh!" said the others, "watch out, Billy, she's got the hots for you!"

"Ah shuddup!" Girlie bent down and started furiously sorting the stuff into heaps.

Then Tina spoke up. "I'm with you, Girlie. Who needs these fullas, eh Suzie." And she began to get stuck into the piles of junk. With a shrug Suzie slowly started in on the smallest lot.

"Might be I'll find that ten cents I lost here," said Waaka. Smart, very smart! And he and Billy started in too.

Oh man. "Come on then," I said to Paul and Eddie, "humour the nut cases."

But when we'd sorted the stuff out finally, I told them, "That's it. I ain't a builder, old style or new. Like Paul said before, you're on your own as far as I'm concerned from now on," and I went down to the pub with Paul and Suzie to cool off.

Must've been only a few days after that I heard Girlie crying as I carne in the door. There was Dad belting her. The old man, he looked really had it, like he had ever since he'd got the notice from the factory. Like all the kaha had drained out of him. After all those years there and then getting that good job, and then - whoosh - the push. But was he laying into Girlie! Good job.

Then I saw that bloody stuck-up Kingi Taylor, Dad's step-brother, in his lawyer's suit and red slippers - his socks might catch on our old boards, eh! Should've guessed that new car taking up half the street would be his. He's the one Dad's family spent all the money on to go to the boarding school and get the good education. Yeah, and here was Dad thirty years later still running hard to catch up to that guy and getting further and further behind. Man, who needed that? "What's this then?" I said when I saw Kingi was sitting looking on.

"Kia ora, a Pere," he said. "Pehea?"

I wasn't having any of his put-down stuff about me being a knownothing Maori. "G'day,'" I told him.

"Your uncle's come to take Girlie home to live with them again," my father said.

"Yeah?" But something funny was going on. I could tell that from the way Girlie was carrying on.

"It's something I can do to help," said that Kingi. "When things are bad a family needs to stick together and help one another."

"Things are bad all right," said Dad, rubbing his unshaved chin with a loud scratching sound. I was pissed off with hearing that old crap. Him and me both on the dole, Mum with her bit of a part-time job - we'd get by till things were better.

Girlie was sniffling and snot and tears were all over the place. Just as well the youngest kids weren't there to see, we'd be drowned.

Just then Girlie gave a jerk of her skinny arm and shot loose from Dad out the door. I tore after her. She raced out the back.

"What's the story?" I grabbed her and held fast.

"I'm not going with that fulla," she said, real staunch she sounded too.

"Why the hell not? You been with them a few years, right up to a couple of years back. What's going on?"

"I can't say. I'm not going, I'm just not and you can't make me, no one's going to do that." She wriggled like an eel trying to get free. She

was wasting her time. We could hear my uncle's voice raised in the house. A shudder went through her, wobbling the flesh on my arm. Who knows how but suddenly I knew. A cold sweat licked up my back. I took a look at Girlie. Oh Jeez!
"You don't mean that ... that he was ... was .... when you were living with him before?"
She stopped dead still, and just nodded. Once.
"You lie, girl?"
She had her head down, shook it.
"But what - I mean just one time, was it?"
She lifted her face and looked at me like I was a dumb little kid. "Lots of times. But I won't go there again, you get that?" And she simply shook my numb hand off her and took off down the road. I stood there. I could feel all my flesh start to quiver. This huge wildness was building in me.
That shit! That sickness! That fake-faced bastard! That - that cannibal! God, he was worse than all those other bastards! Jeez! I flung the door just about off its hinges. I walked up and hit him. Full in the face. I heard my father cry out. The blood on my knuckles felt good. I didn't wipe it off. He stayed where he had fallen over a chair, staring at me, white faced.
I turned to my father. "Girlie's not going with him, " I said.
But he wasn't listening. "Get out, get the hell out of here, you," he was screaming. "You're not my son, you're an animal get yourself out of my house right now, you hear, get out and stay out, you're finished here, for good!" His fist struck me on the shoulder. Mine lifted in reply. But no. I held my arms tight against me. Not that I mustn't hit my father, no matter what. No, I could just about feel a bit sorry for him. No one would ever tell him what this was all about. Couldn't. "Ok, ok." I said, "I will." I guess I must've seemed off my head. My uncle shrank back when I brushed past him. He knew!
"What'd he do that for?" Dad was saying.
"He's bad, that one," I could hear my uncle saying as I went out. I gave his car a chop that just about bust my hand. But the metal didn't even give.
My mind boiled. The money he'd given me a year or so back to stay and try for my school exams - cannibal money!
My feet took me where they wanted.

I found I was shaking some kind of rough gate made of stakes. I blinked. I was on the hill overlooking the creek where they were making that damned wharemoe of Billy's. They'd put up a tall fence of manuka stakes. I rattled the gate again and it opened. I stared.
Jesus! This was something else!
Most of them were there, working. And Waaka looked like he'd been taking lessons at it, giving directions here, looking over something there, real foreman. There didn't seem too many others about though. I saw a couple of mates from hereabouts and, look at that would you, old Potoa of Brown Menace sweating it out in full gang regalia. But I couldn't see much of a house. Just some tops of ponga poking out alongside a dirty great scar of bared earth, and piles of that junk we'd sorted through, and a great long pole held up by some sick-looking supports. Boy!
"Hi," shouted Billy. He looked pleased with himself, anyways.
"Yeah, and where's all that free labour?" I asked.
He looked like he was doing a bit of a shrink there for a minute. "Ah well the old fulla, you know that kaumatua, eh, he didn't like how we were going about it, some of the things - "
"He couldn't jump out of his groove." It was Waaka. "Thought we were going to bring back the last century. Couldn't get it that this was more like the first canoe landfall. He was hung up on stuff like what was men's work and what was women's work and how you did things and so, and I kept saying look we've only got us few and might be some of us'll need this place real soon. So he got hoha and went off and those university guys just took off too, so - "
"But we're ok," said Billy. "Waaka's found out what to do, from his uncle, eh. And we got all we need right here."
"What I reckon," put in Suzie, "is it was finding out Billy's a Raro finally pissed that old man off. "
"Ok," I said, "what's the story now?"
And Waaka explained. I saw it all again, like on a TV screen in my mind - that house, the cooking lean-to and its camp-oven, some chickens, even the Maori loo. Yeah, even a garden and some corns, some kumara. And my sweat going to make something of our own, no one telling us what to do, getting between us and our dreams, using us, ripping us off.
And then I had me an idea. I saw a pile of flax or pandanus mats on the grass. Right out there in front of them all I whipped off my jeans

and wrapped a pliable little mat about my waist. This felt good. I had a sudden flash from school days. "*Tihe mauri ora*!" I yelled.

Then I had to look again. That Girlie! But I stopped myself shouting at her - she'd been ahead of me all along. There she was coming out from behind a bush wearing just the old piupiu Mum kept in the chest at home - a real one, like a piece of fine cloth, not one of those cold-arse modern jobs. And then that Suzie - would be her - was hauling off her gear and rolling herself up in one of the mats, a little green pendant jiggling between her tits. I tell you in a couple of minutes it looked like Captain Cook must be due to come up the creek.

"Ok then," I said. "From here on what we do is what we have, and what we are is what we make, right? And look," I said to Billy, "old time whare or not, I'm going to have us a real brick fireplace, no smoky hole in the ground. You can bet that's what the Otene ancestors would've had if they'd only known. Come all yous, work, or there'll be cold nights under the stars for me!"

Girlie stood looking at me as the others moved to get on with it, only Tina hovering around keeping an eye on us. "Yeah," I told her. "I guess this'll be home for a while now."

And she went off without a word.

It's funny, stuff that seems to float up in my thoughts like bubbles from the bed of that creek while I'm working away here, stuff my aunties told when I was a kid. Like getting birds ready to preserve: snick snick with the knife, push, out come the leg bones, wrench and heave and the body flips inside out, yank and out come the guts and the bone, push and tuck and the bird's back right side out, head still on, now only a little fistful of naked meat ready to be dropped in the can with the others and the boiling fat poured in on top. Well, might be there'll be time for those things yet.

Because, man, we're gonna make it happen here, damn right we will.

GRANDPA AND ME

'What's she doing here?' said my cousin Ricky.
'Shirley wants to come fishing with us,' my grandfather explained.
Ricky pointed to the islands far out in the gulf. 'We're going out there. We'll be away for hours. You'll be in the way!'
'Grandpa?' I appealed.
'Sure you want to come?'
'Please!'
'All right. Have you got everything? Your lunch? Drinks?'
'In this cold box.'
I waded into cold water and climbed over the side. Grandpa pushed the boat into deeper water. There was a scary sideways lurch as he stepped aboard and sat on the middle seat.
'Watch, Shirl,' said Ricky, 'in case you ever have to start an outboard. You click this, then move ... '
'I know.'
'Give a pull on the cord. And ... Oh well, it's sometimes hard to start. Ah! There you are!'
'Why aren't we moving?'
'Ricky,' said Grandpa, 'lower the prop into the water.'
'Oh. Right.'
The boat leaped forward. I had to hold on to the little windscreen as the bow crashed up and down. Spray dashed against my face. I heard Ricky's laugh.
'Ricky!' shouted Grandpa. 'Turn it down! We're not trying to fly!'
Even at the slower speed the boat see-sawed against the waves. My stomach quivered.
Grandpa turned to me. 'Shirley?' He studied my face. 'You be navigator.'
Ricky sneered, 'We'll never find the right place.'
Grandpa took no notice. 'See that point of land? Soon as we're level with it, shout out. And Ricky will turn to starboard ... '
'Where, Grandpa?'
'Turn right,' I said.
' ... and follow the shoreline till I tell you to head out across the channel towards Rangitoto. OK?'
A few minutes later I gave the signal.

'Quite sure?' said Ricky.
'Turn!' I bellowed.
The boat made a wide curve.
Grandpa pulled a carton from under his seat and took up a fillet of fish. A seagull cruising over us cocked an interested eye. Grandpa cut off chunks of half unfrozen fish and slid them on to the wicked looking hooks of a trolling lure.
I reached to help. 'No, Shirley. Too easy to get a hook in your finger.' He stood, feet wide apart, swaying. Just watching him standing upright made me grip the side of the boat. He flung a line out far beyond the outboard motor and tied the end to his seat.
'Ricky, when you change direction, do it gradually. Otherwise we'll have the line around the propeller blades.' A little while later he said, 'Well, look at that.'
The white wake flowed evenly, the thin green line was taut. 'I couldn't steer a better course myself,' said Grandpa.
I faced the front again and watched the almost empty sea rather than Ricky's pleased-with-himself face.
The heat of the sun and the rocking boat were nearly putting me to sleep.
'Shirley!' I jumped. 'When we get opposite a tall white building with a hill of trees behind it, tell Ricky to make the turn. Then line us up exactly half way between the lighthouse and the end of Rangitoto.'
There seemed to be lots of big white buildings. Which one did he mean? I wasn't going to ask and have Ricky jeer at me. Was it that one? No, no hill. Then ... well, maybe ... Or ... ?
The wake began a smooth slow bend. Ricky hadn't even waited for me! I made a quick guess where we were to head. 'Port!' I directed. 'Left! Left I said!' Ricky was going the wrong way on purpose! I could hear him snickering. 'Further left! More. Now right a bit. There!'
'Hold her steady, Ricky,' Grandpa instructed. 'We don't want to miss my favourite fishing spot.'
As Grandpa began hauling in his trolling lines, Ricky cut the motor. Grandpa heaved the anchor over the bow, and we were floating a few hundred metres off a scoria shore. Grandpa checked the fishing line I had baited. I threw the line over. At once I could feel weight at the end of the line. 'A bite!' I gave a tremendous tug to make sure the hook struck.

'Let's feel.' Grandpa shook his head. 'It's only the sinker.' I was waiting for Ricky's laugh. But he was hauling in hand over hand his own line, spraying us with water. 'You beauty!' he shouted. A fish came up out of the water flexing his body from side to side. Ricky dropped it into the bottom of the boat, wrenched free the hook's barb. The thing's tail flapped wildly.

'Good work, Ricky,' said Grandpa.

I jiggled my line impatiently, hoping some passing fish would think my bait was tasty. All I could feel was the sinker's clunk-clunk each time it drifted back to the sea floor.

We sat and sat. I could taste salt on my lips. A splash of water on my leg was drying into a white streak like a snail's track. Occasionally gulls landed on the water to watch us but soon stretched their wings and lumbered into the air.

Were the fish on holiday? 'Must be lunch-time,' I suggested.

Grandpa laughed. 'It's 10.30, Shirley.'

'Morning-tea-time.' I decided.

'You're getting fed up, aren't you?' said Ricky. 'I knew you would.'

'I am not,' I lied.

There was nothing much to watch as I ate: the green of Rangitoto and, a long way off a ship steaming in our direction making for Auckland Harbour. I washed my hands over the side, tried jiggling my line enticingly. We sat silently. Ricky's fish was starting to stink. My legs were getting redder and redder and stinging. One-handed I rubbed more sun cream over them.

Ricky gave a loud sniff. 'What pongs?' He pulled off his shirt.

Why didn't he ever sunburn like me?

'It's all those foreign trawlers and wall-of-death nets,' said Grandpa suddenly.

'What is?' asked Ricky.

'Why we're having no luck. Who'd believe that in the old days they'd come out here and pull in enough to feed the whole hapu?'

I tried to imagine it. I was so hot I couldn't make my brain work. Idly I glanced to see how close the approaching ship was. It was coming right at us! 'Grandpa!' I yelped. 'A ship's going to mow us down!'

Ricky twisted around to look.

Grandpa said, 'It only seems like it, Shirley. We're near the channel the ships use.'

But the ship wasn't turning aside. Its high black rust-flecked bow loomed nearer, higher. I tensed, ready to jump over the side. Grandpa was waving at some men gazing down at us. They smiled back, not caring what happened to us. But, amazingly, the huge ship passed as far away from us as Rangitoto was.

'Look at Shirl,' said Ricky. 'She was so scared she's gone the colour of her cold box.'

I turned away, busied myself with pulling in my line. The bait was mere strings of flesh. Something had been nibbling around the hook! I put on a new piece of fish meat. I hoped the fish wouldn't notice its smell.

The boat was rocking. I glanced up. I was so surprised at what I saw I let my line go. Huge swells were rolling towards our boat from the wake of that ship. I was too scared even to shout a warning. The boat's anchored nose sluggishly swung to face the waves, then rose sharply.

'Roller-coaster ride!' said Ricky. Grandpa chuckled.

Our boat pitched down the other side of the slope of grey water. Another wave came at us and another.

Ricky bent over to hack at more bait. 'Ouch!' He pressed his thumb. The bait knife clattered down, blood-stained.

'What've you done?' Grandpa studied the thumb. I thought he was going to growl at him for being so careless. He just said, 'Wash your hand, Ricky. We're doing no good here. We might as well get you home and have something put on that cut. It's a nasty one.'

Ricky didn't answer, he was holding his hand in the water and gritting his teeth.

'Shirley,' said Grandpa, 'where's your line?'

'I think it's gone over the side,' I had to admit.

'That was a new line!'

I hadn't caught a single fish and I'd lost my line. Grandpa must have been wishing he hadn't let me come.

He stood, ignoring the heaving of the boat, pushed past me to haul at the anchor rope. My top was drenched with cold water by the time the anchor was in. He lurched back to the stern. He pulled the outboard's starter cord once, twice. A huge swell seemed to be carrying us towards the rocks of Rangitoto. Come on, Grandpa, I urged silently. The motor caught. At first the boat could hardly climb the rollers. Grandpa revved the engine. The boat's nose rose and we were thumping over the waves of that ship's wake until we reached calmer sea. Ricky sat nursing his hand.

'You OK, Ricky?' Grandpa checked.
Ricky nodded. Blood leaked down his wrist. My eye fell on the cold box. 'Hey! Put this on, Ricky.' I got out the ice bag that kept things cool. He shoved it aside.
'Do it,' Grandpa instructed. 'It'll stop the bleeding. Good thinking, Shirley.'
The motor coughed. Grandpa twisted the handle. The engine revved, spluttered, died. 'Ricky, can you reach the spare petrol can?'
'Spare?' said Ricky.
'The one I told you to stow under the back seat.'
'Um,' said Ricky, 'I might have forgotten it.'
'Forgotten?' Grandpa felt under his seat. He stared around.
No other boats were anywhere close. His face went red. 'Shove aside,' he snapped at Ricky. 'Shirley, sit beside me. You'll have to row. You'll get sore hands,' he warned. 'We'll have to keep rowing till someone sees us and gives us a tow or till we get home. Can you do it?'
I nodded, picked up an oar, fitted it into its rowlock, held the blade poised above the water,
'Keep in rhythm just as I've shown you. Ready?'
It took a while until we could pull together so that the bow didn't weave from side to side.
Grandpa's face lost its grim expression. He started the song we heard whenever he went rowing. 'Row, row, row ... '
'Your boat,' I joined in.
'You're a chip off the old block,' Grandpa told me. 'We'd have been in trouble without her, wouldn't we, Ricky?'
'How's your hand?' I found breath to ask.
Ricky said not a word to either of us but scowled at the ice bag pressed against his thumb.

WHAKAPAPA

"You want to be a big-head or something?" my grandfather says to me. "You're a little girl at school yet." He won't speak Maori to me ever - even though I ask him to, so that I can practise and learn. Maybe he thinks I'll never understand him.

Right now I want to say, "Hey, I'm in the sixth form, Grandad," but I don't dare, and he makes me feel so small saying all this with my aunties at the back of the room there hearing it.

"To know the whakapapa is not your job. If you want to know it, wait. Then your turn will come. It's not like I'm an old man," he says smoothing his white-sprinkled hair with his hand, "ready to die at any minute. There is time," I can see he's searching round in his mind for something he thinks I'll understand. "You can't run the flag up till the pole is ready! You grow good and strong and get your education - that's your job now."

It is always the same. I come back here, home from the city where we live and I want - yes I really want - to learn from him about our family and hapu that only he can tell me. Because who can teach me these things in the city? But he seems to think I'm just another pakeha-Maori and he's not going to trust sacred things to me. I don't want to be like that, though, I want to know. I want to have my feet on sure ground, I want to know who I am, what paths I can follow. And maybe it's this too - that he really does think I'm just too immature. He's still carrying on as if I'm twelve.

And I have to hold my tongue against my teeth not to say what I'm dying to say, like, 'But even my father too, he doesn't know much yet either' or 'How can anyone be sure that there's so many years left to teach us in?' or even, 'I want to know where I come from - is that so bad?' And I don't ask as I'd done once if I could write some of the stories, the genealogy down at his dictation. It's not that I'm crazy over the family tree, it's more like I know if he'll give me that, he'll be ready to share some of the other things - you know, like customs, beliefs, ceremonials, the stories of our people's history, our proverbs and so.

"I know some families have a family book," I had told him, "they've got it all down so it can't get lost." He got really mad at me. "That's a pakeha notion," he said, "write it down and forget it. Put it in a book and that's it! How can you get the real things down in black squiggles?

Are you so clever you can find the words to write all the feelings, all the thoughts that are as delicate yet as strong as a spider's web, all the things your face and your eyes show as you speak, all the tapu essences? Books! They are cemeteries!" His face got so flushed that my aunty came and shooed me away. Other times when I've asked about these sorts of things (you can tell I'm persistent, eh) he'd just tap my knuckles and say, "Pretty girl." Yeah, that's what I was first and foremost to grandad - a female. Good for the kitchen! A handy young hui helper! And that would make me mad. It's tough I can tell you being wild with someone you at the same time love and respect so much!

Well, this is my grandfather's place. So I obediently go back to helping in the kitchen. And I don't say anything to my mother either, she can't seem to understand how strongly I feel, how frustrated and miserable my grandfather's 'No' makes me whenever we come back here - and that's not so often, either, because it's so far to come.

We could not believe it at first for a long time, the news of their deaths. A whole carload on the way to a hui, off the road, down the steep bank to the river. My grandfather dead, my uncle, my aunty, old Sammy my step uncle. Old Mrs Heta in the car with them. All gone. Lying there dead for hours maybe till they were found. I couldn't think about that. And so soon after we'd been to visit with them.

But it isn't just them being gone, these people so precious to me, that cuts me. The idea sticks in my mind and won't move that it is also like the history of my family, the knowledge of the roots of people, all the most valued things that are gone with them, part of them. Just as dead and gone and lost as those old Egyptians and Romans that the teachers used to tell us about. No, more than them. It was like a family's whole savings buried and nobody knows any more where it is. It's like you've lost the steering column of your car. (That's the sort of thing my grandfather'd say!) Somehow I feel it is my fault in a way. Not only that if I'd really kept hassling him he'd have taught me something. No, it's also that I feel guilty I ever had the thought that an accident could do what it has done.

But this goes out of my mind. For there is the tangi, there are the people to let know, there is the emptiness of that house in the country by the marae to face and to get used to.

I find that I am the one who has to drive into the township and register the deaths and do some of the other things that the law makes you do while you're still numbed with grief.

A pakeha fulla comes out of an office as I am going to leave. I vaguely remember seeing him once or twice at hui when pakehas were represented for some reason or other. "I'm sorry to hear of your loss, Miss Waaka," he says, "your grandfather in particular will be sorely missed. He was a regular authority on Maori things. A most fascinating person." He hesitates and looks really sharply at me. "Maybe you'd like to come and see this?" He doesn't sound too sure. We go into a little dark room crowded with books and bundles of papers. He takes an old book big as an office account book out of a cupboard and with it a dusty book, a real old fashioned large printed book with gold bits on its thick covers. "The man who had this job before my time here kept this up. It's from the records of the Maori Land Court when it used to have dealings in this area. It's been useful in the past for your people that we had it, you know. It's a family tree, I suppose. Some of it, anyway."

Pages of it. Right back a hundred years - no, no, much more - pages of names going right back when. "I think the old fellow who recited this lot originally to the court claimed it went back to the creation of the world!" He smiled. "My predecessor kept it up all the time he was working here. Suppose it's not of much interest to anyone these days, though. "

I look. I just cannot speak. I am so stupid with amazement.

"Oh, and this book. It's not in many libraries nowadays. Part of it contains some of the traditions of the people who lived in this area. Collected about the turn of the century - perhaps earlier - by quite a famous authority of the time on Maori culture. I wouldn't know how accurate they are, but they're here in Maori and English. I imagine they were supposed to go with the family tree thing."

All in a book! Some quizzy pakeha had them all in a book all the time!

"Possibly," he says looking at me again - I think maybe my mouth is hanging open by this time - "you'd like to have a good look?" I must be gripping them tight because he says, "They can always be copied on the copier machine. I can't let them out of the office, you see."

"Ok," is all I can say.

I am suddenly afraid. Perhaps you're not wrong, Grandad - these are the words all right - but can the words still speak to us all that they mean?
And shakily I sit down with my ancestors heavy on my knee. And pray that they can still talk to me and that I can understand.

IF YOU LIKED THIS ....

whanau is one of a three part series of short stories by Eternal Gadd

A collection of eleven short stories on lust, longing, love and loss by a master story teller from Aotearoa. Meet Frank, the would be Romeo, bumbling his way into a honey trap, teenage Tania caught up in something she doesn't know how to deal with, John giving lessons to his teacher and Gabrielle struggling to come to terms with who she is. All of them caught in the web of Desire.

Whanau - 'family' in Maori - is a collection of fourteen short stories about family, friends, fears and faith. Lovers, mothers, grandparents and friends all trying to build that single most important aspect of humanity - love and the bonds of connection that make a family. They struggle against the odds, against the attempts of others to stop them, and against their own frailties and inabilities. You cannot fail to be moved by these gritty, authentic stories.

A home is what everyone desires - a place to truly belong, to be yourself, a shelter from the world, a place of certainty. Here in this collection of fourteen short stories, find people (and one dog) struggling to carve out a place for themselves. Meet Tokerau torn between her family history and her modern reality, Hoani and Pati seeking out Jerusalem, Nanny Paora trying to preserve her slice of land from the clutches of the Government and Mae who needs to know if she can say her home is truly hers.

ABOUT THE AUTHOR

Hallard Press is a boutique publisher based in Aotearoa, New Zealand and this book is one of a triology of collected short stories produced under the author name Eternal Gadd which is actually a psuedoname representing works from three generations of Gadds - all of them called David.

DA Gadd

David wrote mainly about growing up in New Zealand in the early years of the 20th Century when the family lived on the rural outskirts of the Auckland province. He was one of 12 children in a madcap family. He lived with a father intent on pursuing money making schemes and dreams into which he dragged the whole family with very mixed results and a long suffering wife. The family, as if not large enough of itself, was always being further enlarged by dogs, horses and the odd characters they encountered. As an adult David served in the Pacific during World War II, where he sustained a lasting injury. He was a talented writer of music, an amateur historian, always enthusiastic to jump in a car and travel around our beautiful country and a loving father and grandfather.

David Bernard Gadd

The main author of these short stories is DB Gadd, known to all as Bernard Gadd. He was a prolific writer of short stories, novels, plays and poetry, an editor of anthologies and literary journals and a publisher. All this, remarkably, was in his spare time. His main focus was as a teacher, the head of English at a college where he engaged in pioneering work in the classroom - this was the genesis of his writing, when he realised there were few authors writing stories relevant to the real lives of his students, who were mainly Maori and Pasifika teenagers living in a low socio-economic area of Auckland. So he began to write stories himself, designed to encourage literacy amongst students left behind by mainstream education. He engaged them by reflecting the experiences of their own lives in contrast to the sanitised versions of family life they were fed by most media. It worked, he captured their imagination and showed them the power of reading. His commitment to multi-culturalism also saw him foster a new generation of talented emerging Maori and Pacific writers and poets. He founded Hallard Press.

DS Gadd

Although he made his living writing, he was only ever a dabbler in writing of any worth. Instead he mainly concentrated on continuing the dubious Gadd tradition of a having a mad family surrounded by even crazier animals - all the while living with a beautiful, talented and (of course) long suffering wife, two gorgeous children and a variety of dogs, cats, rodents and goats.

OTHER BOOKS YOU MIGHT LIKE

Laya

Kidnapped by fugitives, teenage girl Laya is forced to become an apprentice to the dreaded, aging magician Langi. Frightened, lonely and angry she gradually accepts her place amongst these people and in the end, utterly unexpected, the future of them all is dropped within her hands. Can she decide for the best? The novel is set four thousand years ago amongst the sea voyaging ancestors of the Polynesians of the Pacific Islands. Fast paced and authentic, the story grips you and takes you there on the great canoes that settled the vast Pacific.

The more poetry you read, the better you write

A collection of essays on why reading poetry is something everyone who writes should do - every student struggling with essays, every businessman writing reports, every would be novelist - because reading poetry can make you a better writer. It includes essays on the haiku, dispenses with the complaints of rule-makers who try to restrain the haiku in moribund ancient formulae and urges every poet to try haiku - delivering maximum effect with minimum waffle.

CONTACT THE PUBLISHER

Thank you for buying this Hallard Press book.
We welcome feedback . You can get in touch via:

hallardpress@gmail.com

or follow our updates on

facebook.com/HallardPress

www.ingramcontent.com/pod-product-compliance
Ingram Content Group UK Ltd.
Pitfield, Milton Keynes, MK11 3LW, UK
UKHW020235250726
13967UKWH00001B/384